Widowmakers

A JTF 13 Novel

By:

William Joseph Roberts

Three Ravens Publishing
Chickamauga, GA

Published by Three Ravens Publishing
threeravenspublishing@gmail.com
P.O. Box 851 Chickamauga, Ga 30707
https://www.threeravenspublishing.com

Publishers Note: This is a work of fiction. Names, characters, places, and incidents are a product of the author's imagination. Locales and public names are sometimes used for atmospheric purposes. Any resemblance to actual people, living or dead, or to businesses, companies, events, institutions, or locales is completely coincidental.

<u>Credits:</u>
Widowmakers was written by William J. Roberts

Widowmakers by: William J. Roberts, Cannon Publishing, 1st edition, 2019
Widowmakers by: William J. Roberts, Three Ravens Publishing, 2nd edition, 2020

Trade Paperback ISBN: 978-1-951768-17-1

Legacy Trade Paperback ISBN: 978-1-951768-32-4

Authors Note:

As with anything I do, there's usually a great deal of research involved. This particular story and the setting sent my evil mind squirrels to task, and down the rabbit holes of the internet we went. Now the upside to all this research is the number of new folks I have met, (in Facebook groups mostly), and because of the amount of time I took out of these folks' busy days, I'd like to give them a special little shout out.

Thank you to the members of the Northrop P-61 Black Widow Facebook group, The B-25 Mitchell Fans Facebook group, the Mid-Atlantic Air Museum, and the wonderful folks down at the Museum of Aviation at Warner Robbins Air Force Base for letting me turn wrenches on an actual B-17 Flying Fortress. A special thank you goes out to Michael Woods for all the information he bestowed upon me about the aircraft they have in the museum. (Dude is a serious fountain of knowledge.)

This particular story was a fun change of pace into a time period I've wanted to write in for some time. The fact that I was able to take part in my own backstory and turn a lowly wrench-turning crew chief (aircraft mechanic) from the 2nd pursuit squadron into a hero was pretty damned cool. Knowing there was a chance other aircraft-loving gearheads could possibly be reading this really drove my need to know the finer details about the specific aircraft featured in this story.

Last, but never least, a huge loving thank you goes to my beloved wife, Meg. She is my rock, my sounding board, and my voice of reason when the squirrels send me spiraling in too many directions. Thank you, babe.

Table of Contents

Chapter 1

“I don't know about the rest of youse guys, but I know exactly what I'm going to do when I get back to the States,” Private First Class Russo said in a thick Brooklyn accent. He shuffled through a handful of well-worn playing cards. “I've got four books,” he said, then looked to the soldier to his right. “Your turn, Burns.”

“I've got two,” Private Burns said as he tapped his hand level and laid the cards face down on the table. “Your turn, Gershowitz.” Burns reached under the table and retrieved an unopened bottle of beer, popping the cap loose on the edge of the table with a quick slap.

“Well, don't leave us hanging in suspense, Russo,” Corporal Gershowitz said. “Three books for me,” he said, placing his cards on the table. He pulled out a pack of Lucky Strikes from his shirt pocket, slid a cigarette from the opened end, then mouthed it and lit it with the smoldering stub of his previous smoke. “I think you're just full of shit and like to hear your own lips flap, Russo.”

Russo scoffed, “You're the one that's full of shit, Gershowitz.”

Gershowitz snatched the beer from Burns before he'd taken the first sip. He upended the beer and emptied the bottle in two gulps, then let out a loud, wet belch.

"Hey, asshole! That was my beer!" Burns yelled.

"Not anymore it isn't!" I laughed, nursing one of my own rare and coveted drinks.

"Very funny, Sarge," Burns said. "Asshole."

"Watch it, Burns," I warned. "That could be considered disrespect of a non-commissioned officer." I tapped a crooked camel cigarette from my crumpled package. Lifting the glass of an old kerosene lamp, I lit the smoke from the oily flame. Dust motes launched from the narrow shelf where the lamp sat and floated carelessly about the only source of light in the old barn as I exhaled. The sweet smell of the tobacco overpowered the smell of dry hay and livestock.

"Sorry, Sergeant Sullivan," Burns said as he shuffled through his hand, avoiding eye contact with me. "Won't happen again, Sarge."

"Don't worry about it, Burns," I said with a chuckle and took a long draw from the unfiltered cigarette. "I'm just messing with you, Private. Nothing to worry yourself about." I flashed a mischievous smile at him and took another sip of my warming beer.

"Yeah, he likes to fuck with the rookies, Burnsie," Russo said. "Hey, Gershowitz, tell Burnsie here what the Sarge did to you when you first reported for duty."

"Piss off, Russo. Are we going to play spades or what? Christ's sake," Gershowitz said, uncomfortably shifting.

"Oh hell, here we go again," Staff Sergeant Henderson said and folded up the letter he'd just been working on. "Why in the hell do you fellas have to get Russo riled up like this? You know he won't shut up for hours once he gets started."

"Oh, har har freaking har! Very funny, Staff Sergeant," Russo said.

"Might as well go ahead and tell Burns the story before your head explodes," I said, then took a long drink of the warm but tasty beer. We'd acquired a case of the freshly bottled sunshine from a local brewer earlier in the day, in exchange for a gallon of diesel fuel and a pair of size nine combat boots Russo had recovered from a German scout we'd caught snooping around camp the week before.

We'd been assigned as a detachment of the 2nd Pursuit Squadron to Forward Air Base Jackson. Our orders were simple as an intercept unit; chase down and destroy any German bomb raiders before they could reach allied forces, or escort our bomb groups across the German lines as requested by HQ. They'd originally issued us six Curtiss P-40 Warhawks, three Lockheed P-38 Lightnings, and a lone North American P-51 Mustang.

Only a few days earlier a baker's dozen of Northrop P-61A Black Widows arrived on our doorstep, fresh off the assembly line in the States. Without notice, the squadron of aircraft landed, rolled to a stop, and parked in a neat and tidy formation near the commandeered barn of our quaint little airfield in northern France. The Army Corps of Engineers had surveyed the area north of what remained of the village of Evrecy and deemed it as suitable. Decades of livestock grazing had compacted the soil well enough for use by smaller aircraft.

In hindsight, it would have been nice if the engineers had offered a few solutions to removing a steadfast herd of sheep from the path of an incoming aircraft without the use of brute force or a truck. The herdsmen didn't care for our routine use of the .50 cals to clear the runway, but sometimes you gotta do what you gotta do. *If that's the least of our problems, we're doing pretty damned good*, I thought and took another swig of my lukewarm beer.

"Well, you see," Russo said, "Sarge here asked Burnsie if he was musically inclined in any way. Burns said he was, and that he'd played a bit of guitar growing up. Then Sarge asked if he'd like the chance to play an Army Banjo out back to help the unit out of a serious bind. Being the kiss-ass that he is, Burnsie jumped all over the opportunity. Then the next thing you know, Sarge here handed him a shovel and told him to start digging the next shitter pit out back of the barn." Russo laughed, slapping his knees.

"Can we play cards already?" Burns looked to Stewart. "Isn't it your turn, Private?"

"I can get eight books," Private Stewart said, then leaned back in his chair.

"Whoa! We've got ourselves a big spender right here!" Gershowitz shouted.

"You know you're going to put us in the hole even further if you're bluffing again," Burns said.

"Why would I bluff?" Stewart dropped his hand face down on the table.

"Cause you're full of shit, Stewie. That's why," Gershowitz said. "Play your card already, Russo.

"Oh, ha ha ha," Stewart said, flashing a middle finger in Gershowitz's direction.

Russo fanned out his cards and sorted through the hand. "Keep your shorts on, I'm thinking." He carefully rearranged the position of the cards, then chose one from the center of the hand, and placed a six of clubs face up on the table.

"What the hell kind of play is that, you stupid Dago?" Gershowitz shouted. "Are you *trying* to lose this round for us?"

"No more than you are, you freaking big nose!" Russo shouted back.

"Cool it, both of you," I said. "You start that bullshit arguing again, and you'll have the captain and the rest of the flyboys down here chewing our asses."

"Fine," Russo said, shifting in his seat. "I'll keep it down so the precious pilots up in the hayloft get their beauty rest.

"So, spit it out already," Gershowitz said, changing the subject. "What's this *secret* plan of yours, Russo?"

"Oh, yeah. I almost forgot about that. See, it's simple really. Even for a bunch of apes like youse guys." Russo laid his cards face down and straightened the collar of his fatigue shirt. "As soon as I get back to the States, I'm going straight home to kiss my Ma. Then I'm going to go out and find me a good, God-fearing Italian girl to bring home. Nothing against the Jewish or the Sicilian girls back in Brooklyn. I mean, there's more than a few hot numbers I wouldn't mind taking out a time or two. But Ma is just that sorta particular when it comes to marriage and prospective grandchildren. The woman I choose has gotta be from good, wholesome stock, ya' know."

"What would your Ma say if you were to bring home a French girl? Especially if it's true love," Private Stewart said.

"Ya know, I'm not honestly sure, come to think of it," Russo said. "Ma's never really said much of anything about the Frenchies back in Little Paris on the west side of Brooklyn. Granted, there aren't any that I know of from back in the old neighborhood, so that might be part of it."

"Well, hell, Russo," Private Steward said. "You can have the pick of the litter, then. There's a whole herd of soft and fuzzy French girls out at the end of the runway.

"Oh, ha ha, smartass," Russo said. "That would be more up Sergeant Sullivan's alley," he said with a nod toward me.

"Best watch yourself, Private," I said, then turned up my beer and emptied the bottle. "That was good, Burns. Thank you." I set the bottle down on the table and headed for the door.

"Where you going, Sarge?"

"I'm stepping out before it gets too deep in here." I slipped out of the barn through the small side door.

The moon hung high and full in the clear July sky. A warm, lavender-scented breeze blew in from the south, across vast fields of the fragrant flowering bush. Rounding the rear corner of the barn, I made my way to the tree line of a small copse of hardwoods. Nature's rhythmic night songs of love struck me as a competition between the crickets of the underbrush and the frogs from a nearby pond.

I finished my business and started back to the barn. Stopping outside the small side door, I pulled another cigarette from the nearly empty package, lighting it from the previous one. I field stripped the stub, making sure to stomp out the still smoldering ember, when I heard a strange grating screech from the airfield. It was like the sound made by scraping nails across a chalkboard, but mingled with an odd metallic twang. Cautiously I approached the front of the barn and crouched in the shadow of the structure. My breath caught in my throat as I waited, motionless. I watched for the slightest hint of movement among the small squadron of mixed aircraft parked to the side of the open pasture. Twisting metal screeched and popped from the nose landing gear bay of *Jumpin' Jess*, one of the unit's newly-issued P-61 Black Widow pursuit aircraft.

Originally, Russo saw her tail number, 42-39212 and wanted to name her Double-Deuce, complete with a five-card poker hand-painted across her nose containing two pairs of twos and an ace of spades in the center due to the last three digits of her tail number. Instead, I chose to name her after this blonde bombshell of a gal I knew from back home. We'd dated for a short time before I enlisted and got shipped out to Boot. I wasn't without a fair bit of artistic talent, so I took it upon myself to paint a likeness of Jess, topless in a torn and tattered dress, leaning back against a still and holding a BAR, or Browning Automatic Rifle, across her bare chest. She held it close, snuggled deep into the ample painted cleavage.

I doubt I'll ever get that particular image out of my mind. It was one hell of a night spent on the side of Lookout Mountain in McLemore Cove, Georgia, guarding one of her father's stills from his competitors. One thing led to another, and before you knew it, we were both pouring sweat in the sweltering August night. And anyone who's spent time in Georgia in the middle of August knows there's no such thing as cool during that time of the year.

Something large had rolled in the underbrush about fifty yards down the hill from us. I'd jumped to my feet and grabbed the shotgun, ready for a fight. When I glanced back at her, that was the exact image that had been forever burned into my brain. Come to think of it, I don't know of any red-blooded man who'd want that image out of his mind. It turned out the noise we'd heard was actually a federal revenuer, and not one of her father's competitors from over the mountain in Fort Payne. We detained him until the next morning, when her father came up to the site and sent us back to the house for some breakfast.

Something grunted loudly and pulled me out of the fond memories of Jess. Instinctively I reached down to loosen the strap over the Colt Army revolver that hung on my right hip. My father had passed it down to me before I'd shipped out for the war. He'd carried it during the Great War, his father before him had carried it during the Spanish War, and his father before him carried it during the War of Northern Aggression. Great Grandad Jacob had gotten it from the cold, dead hands of a Union officer during the battle of Chickamauga. So, my father thought it was only fitting that I should carry it into the next war and make our family proud. I looked in the direction of the noise and saw something moving about in the shadows of *Jumpin' Jess's* nose landing gear bay.

Widowmakers

Probably just a possum or something, I thought, then wondered to myself if they had possums in France. The thing jerked and grunted in time with the sound of popping sheet metal. I put the strap back over the revolver and secured it in place. Without taking my eyes off the aircraft, I reached down into the wooden tool tray Burns had left sitting at the corner of the barn earlier in the day. The inch and a half open-ended wrench I found was heavy in my grip but would work fine for running a critter out of the landing gear.

I crouched low as I crept across the field to the aircraft. I could hear a subtly wet slurping sound that reminded me of a dog gnawing on a bone coming from the wheel well. Leaning down, I peered upward into the darkness of the bay. Nothing moved, but I could hear the faint sound of a raspy wheezed breathing. I shifted my position to the aft of the nose gear and saw a flinching movement within the darkness.

"I've spent entirely too much time maintaining this bird for you to go and chew up her wiring," I said to the thing in the darkness. "Don't know what you are, but you gotta go."

I shifted again to get a better view before reaching blindly into the area. Retrieving my grandfather's zippo from my pocket, I flicked it open and lit the battered lighter against my pant leg in one swift motion.

"Let's see if we can't get a better look at you." As I held the lighter near the opening, the thing moved. Claws scratched across the metal of the compartment as the thing scrabbled between the nose strut's upper mount and the forward bulkhead of the bay. I shifted to the front side of the strut, holding the lighter above my head to get a better look at the thing without sticking my head up into the area. It moved, and I caught a quick glimpse of a nearly hairless, fleshy-brown section of hide. It had alternating stripes of darker and lighter skin like you'd see on a tabby cat. It shifted again as I moved the light around to get a better look.

"Well, I guess you're just an old mangy cat, ain't you," I mumbled to myself as I tried to get a better look at the thing. "I don't want to kill you if I don't have to. Come on out of there, and I'll let you go on your way. We'll just let bygones be bygones."

Flipping the heavy steel wrench in the air, I caught it by the open crescent-like end. Shifting my position to the rear of the strut, I straddled the nose wheel and sat down to get a better angle, then poked the tapered shaft end of the wrench into the space and immediately froze in place.

The thing that stared back at me was unlike anything I'd ever seen in my twenty-two short years on this earth. Beady black eyes glared back at me from behind a long, wrinkled snout. It stank worse than the wet musky stink of a hound at the end of a chase. Viscous yellow drool seeped from between hundreds of needle-like teeth. Its ragged and torn jackrabbit-like ears shook like one of those tiny rat dogs I'd seen rich ladies carry around in purses with them up in Chattanooga. It let out a low, hissing growl similar to the sound I'd heard a trapped possum make. Reflexively I stabbed at the creature with the end of the wrench as it lunged at me from the wheel well. It clawed and hissed, gnashing and snapping in my direction. I slid off the nose tire and moved to the side, backing out of the way of the thing as it clambered over the top of the strut. Suddenly it let out a hoarse, barking cry and leaped for me.

Without even thinking, I brought the wrench around, connecting with the side of the thing's head. It writhed about on the ground, striking blindly at the air around it. I flipped the wrench back over and brought the crescent-shaped end down on the thing's head, over and over again. It squealed in pain, lashing out at the wrench. I brought the makeshift weapon down once more on top of its head, and the creature went limp. Black ichor seeped from the wounds I'd inflicted on the thing. A long, gurgling gasp escaped from its motionless form.

Rushing back to the toolbox, I retrieved a pair of long-handled pliers and picked the thing up by the three-clawed toes of its right foot. I held it up in the moonlight, examining its long, muscular form, then retrieved my lighter. I struck the lighter's flint and held up the creature again. It was at least two feet long when stretched out and was covered in fine fuzz that was an overall fleshy brown color with darker brown stripes. Heavy black claws tipped both its toes and the three human-like fingers on each of its hands.

"I don't know what the hell you are, but there sure as hell aren't any of you back in the hills of Tennessee," I said, then turned back, heading for the barn.

"Hey, Russo," I said as I slipped into the side door of the barn. "I think one of those illegitimate kids of yours came looking for their daddy." I held the creature up in the dim lamplight for all to see.

Stewie crossed himself and mumbled something about demons, along with a quick "Hail Mary".

"Wow, Russo. As ugly as you are, this thing's mom must have been a two-bag dog," Gershowitz chided.

"Damn, Russo," Staff Sergeant Henderson said with a laugh. "I knew you were desperate, but damn, man."

"Piss off," Russo said to Henderson, flipping him the finger, then paused and retracted his finger. "Sarge..."

Burns walked over and cautiously examined the motionless creature. "What is it?"

"No clue," I said. "But in the morning when we have some light, we need to take a good look in the nose well of *Jumpin' Jess*. I found it up behind the nose strut, chewing on the wires or something."

"Is it a rabbit, maybe?" Henderson stepped closer, pushing his glasses up onto the bridge of his nose.

"It can't be a rabbit," Russo said. "There ain't no rabbit I've ever seen with claws like that."

"You've never been to Texas, then, have you, Private?" Henderson said as he examined the thing.

The sudden sound of shearing metal reverberated through the night outside the barn.

We all turned and looked in the direction of the large barn door and wondered at the sound of breaking glass and popping sheet metal hidden behind them.

"What in the hell?" Henderson said as he stood and walked over to the large door at the front of the barn. He lifted the latch and opening the barn door, then froze. "What the hell…"

A cold loathing washed over me as I peered past the staff sergeant's shoulder. The creature and the pliers I held it in fell to the ground as I once again reached down and loosened the leather strap securing the Colt Army revolver in its holster. I watched, dumbfounded as figures milled about in the shadows of the airfield. Before I could react, a fuel tank at the end of the runway suddenly erupted in a fireball that had to have stretched over a hundred feet into the moonlit sky. The flames illuminated the area and the hundreds of creatures that swarmed over the aircraft of our quaint little airfield in Northern France.

Chapter 2

"Jaysus, Joseph, and Mary. Sergeant! I think we've got ourselves a live one!" My head pounded at the sound of a voice with a heavy Irish accent. I heard a low mumbling grunt as something cold and hard poked me uncomfortably in the ribs.

"Eh, I'm not so sure about that," another voice said, this one with a heavy Wisconsin accent, as something poked me again. "Could just be like a snake after you've cut off its head, and it keeps squirming and trying to bite you."

"I'm pretty sure he's alive, Grabowski," the Irishman said. "See, look there. I can see his chest moving like he's breathing."

"Could be one of those things crawled up inside him and it'll bust out of his chest when we get too close."

"What the hell are you two standing around for?" another voice shouted. "Start digging him out of the debris already. For Pete's sake, am I going to have to tell you how to wipe your own asses next?"

"Oh, right. Suppose we should, shouldn't we?" the Irishman said.

"Yeah, you should. Now get to work, both of you, before I write you up for a court-martial."

"Sure thing, Sarge," the Wisconsin voice said with a sigh. "Come on, let's get this over with, O'Brian."

"Aye. Suppose we might as well," the Irishman said.

Panicked thoughts flashed through my mind of a terrifying night spent in an abandoned mine when I was twelve as something heavy shifted and pressed down against my chest. We'd been living on a small farmstead near the base of Sand Mountain at the time. The summers in Tennessee were long, hot, and jam-packed full of boredom and chores. Any opportunity the kids of the area could find to get together out in the woods for a little adventure, we did. Allen Lasley, son of a miner and one hell of a carpenter, had borrowed a pair of his daddy's carbide lamps and told us about this old abandoned coal mine his dad had taken him to that was only a mile or so around the west side of the mountain from us. So, like any other bored and adventure-starved youngins, we went to have ourselves a look. Sure enough, it didn't look like anyone had worked the mine in years. Weeds had grown up around the entrance, along with privet brush that all but blocked the opening from view. We all hem-hawed about and spent well over an hour *inspecting* the entrance before Allen got fed up with waiting. He struck the flint on his light and stormed into the mine alone.

Reluctantly, we followed him down into the mine. The floor gradually sloped downward at a steady angle as we silently trudged into the darkness. We'd stopped at an intersection of six tunnels and began to argue which way to go next. Allen had the bright idea to mark the wall of the passage we'd come down by scratching an arrow that pointed up the tunnel with a small rock fragment he'd found on the ground. The back and forth bickering continued until Allen shouted at the top of his lungs and kicked one of the nearby supports out of frustration. Well, I just happened to be standing directly under the section of roof being supported by a rotted and ancient support beam. I don't really remember much after that, until I woke up in my bed surrounded by my friends, family, and Doc Adair, who'd traveled all the way from downtown Chattanooga. Apparently the ceiling had collapsed after Allen's little tantrum and dropped a few tons of stone on top of me. I just happened to be lucky enough that it fell in such a way as to trap me within a tiny pocket. At some point, one of the others had gotten our parents and dug me out of the collapsed tunnel. We'd all learned a valuable lesson and never went exploring through abandoned mines ever again.

The weight pressing down on my chest suddenly shifted to my left and lifted away as the world around me exploded with a bright light that warmed my clammy, sweat-drenched face. I raised my arm, covering my eyes to block the blinding light.

"I'll bloody well be damned. He *is* alive," the Irishman said.

"Told you he was alive," the second voice said matter-of-factly.

"Would you look at that, Ski," the Irishman said. "He's got three of those things impaled on that wrench."

"Grab his arm, Grabowski. Help me get him out of here."

"Sure thing, Sarge," said Grabowski, the second voice.

I felt myself being lifted and carried as if in a dream. My stomach lurched. I coughed and dry heaved without the slightest bit of release.

"Give me your canteen, O'Brian."

I glanced up, after retching for what I hoped was the last time, to see a tall but lean individual reaching out to a stocky redheaded man in a bowler hat. My face reflexively itched at the sight of the man's dry, bushy mutton chops.

"Um...that might not be the best of ideas, sir. He's a bit green around the gills already, don't ya think?" O'Brian protectively clutched at his canteen.

The tall man turned back and looked at something behind me. I could see the staff sergeant stripes that adorned either sleeve of his uniform. He adjusted the sling strap of his Thompson submachine gun where it hung across his shoulder.

"What about you, Ski? Is your canteen full of water, or whiskey?"

Grabowski chuckled lightly. "Sure would be nice if it was full of whiskey," he mused.

A tall, dark-haired man came into view, standing to my right. "Here ya go, Cap," he said, the large goiter on his neck bobbing as he talked. He handed the canteen to the staff sergeant, who knelt on the ground beside me.

"Drink slow, laddy," O'Brian said. "You've taken a wee beating about the head, from the looks of it."

"Here," the staff sergeant said as he popped the cap off the canteen and helped me to lean up. "You're lucky as hell you didn't burn to death, kid. Looks like you were blown clear of the structure by an explosion. Can you tell me who you are and what happened, Sergeant?"

I gladly took the canteen and turned it up, the cool water soothing my dry throat.

"Whoa now, son! Sip slowly, unless you want to start puking again. You're a bit banged up, but otherwise it looks like you still have all your parts."

I nodded as I took another swig. Swishing the water around my parched mouth, I spit, then took another sip. "The name is Sullivan," I said. "Grady Sullivan. Lead mechanic of the 2nd Pursuit Squadron, Forward Detachment Baker."

The staff sergeant extended his hand and smiled. "Craig Rustay," he said. "325th Glider Infantry Regiment, 82nd Airborne Division."

I took the proffered hand and glanced up at the young-looking man. "Flying coffins, huh?" I smiled and leaned up, using the sergeant's hand to pull myself forward. "And I thought those assholes from the 82nd Airborne were crazy. You must qualify as certified bat shit crazy to take a ride in one of those heaps."

Rustay grunted a laugh. "Yeah," he said, sighing. "You could say that. Can you tell us what happened?"

I started to scratch the side of my head, then jerked away from my own hand as pain shot across the side of my head.

"I wouldn't mess with that too much before we can get you cleaned up." Rustay produced a handkerchief from his pocket, wetted it, and began patting it against the side of my head. "Do you remember what happened?"

"Well," I said, trying to remember what had led to my current situation. "The last thing I can remember…"

"Woot! Hey! I think we're in luck. We should still be able to get this bird in the air! Just some cosmetic damage, from the looks of it."

I leaned left to glance around the staff sergeant. An individual dressed in the khaki tan of a Marine flight suit stomped at an upper cowling panel from the number one engine nacelle of *Jumpin' Jess*.

"What in the hell do you think you're doing? Get your grubby dick beaters off her, and get your sorry jarhead ass off my plane!" I reached for the revolver at my hip, only to find the gun missing and holster empty. "Hey! I said get the hell off her!" Scrambling to my feet, I pushed past the staff sergeant and sprinted for *my* aircraft. The Marine walked to the end of the wing and bounced.

"Don't stand on the wingtips! Asshole!" The Marine ducked, lying flat on top of the wing, as I began throwing rocks at him. "I haven't spent hours upon hours turning wrenches on *Jess* just for you to come along and stomp all over her back!"

"Sergeant Sullivan. Hey, Sergeant!" Rustay snapped his fingers in front of my face as he shook me. "Calm down, Sergeant. That's Warrant Officer Pierce. He's with us."

"I don't give two shits if he's MacArthur himself. Get off my plane!" I threw another rock at the Marine pilot.

"If you know what's good for you, you'll stand down right now, Sergeant! If that plane is the only flyable aircraft on this field, then we're going to board her and fly ourselves back to one of the rear base camps, regardless of what you want. Is that understood?"

I looked around at the devastation wrought across the quaint little airfield. Wisps of smoke danced about the charred remains of the lone P-51 Mustang and two of the P-38 Lightnings.

"My planes! *Holy shit*...what happened to my planes?"

"The things didn't leave us much to work with," the Marine said. He looked around from the top of the plane, hands on his hips. "Give me a few to check the systems on this bird, and I'll let you know if we can get her airborne.

Rustay tapped me on the arm and pointed toward *Jumpin' Jess.* "Do you think we could fit all seven of us in there?"

By this point, I was fuming. I'm sure he saw my jaw muscles flexing as I fought to bite my tongue and keep myself from saying something to an officer that I'd regret later. I glanced over and let out a reluctant breath.

"Yeah, we could all fit, but it sure as hell won't be comfortable. We'll have to dump some of the ammo, too. We at least need to adjust her weight to make sure we can get off the ground."

"Good." Rustay smiled and slapped me across the shoulder. "Think you're up to giving Pierce a hand getting her flight worthy?"

"You mean the jarhead flyboy up there on my girl's back?"

"That would be him."

Letting out a long, reluctant sigh, I looked at him with a sidelong glance. "Don't suppose I have much of a choice, do I?"

"Not really." He chuckled. "Alright! Listen up you apes!" Staff Sergeant Rustay climbed on top of the remains of the old barn and stood in full view of the troops. "Gather anything useable. Guns, ammo, rations, meds. Grabowski, you and Doyle search the bodies, take anything usable, and police their tags while you're at it."

"What about my guys?" I stepped around in front of the Rustay. "We can't just leave them here like this."

Rustay laughed with a slight smile. "Well, we can, and we will, Sergeant. We need to get back to someone in charge and report what we've found here, and down the road a few miles back."

I'm sure my face twisted with a look of confusion.

Rustay rotated the Thompson so it hung behind his back and pulled a cigar from his breast pocket. He bit the tip off one end of the cigar and lightly chewed at the other, wetting it.

"You still haven't told me what happened here, Sergeant." He patted at his pockets, searching for something.

I produced my worn Zippo lighter, struck it on my leg, and held it out for him. "I found one of those things messing around on the nose gear of *Jess* there," I said with a sideways nod toward the aircraft. "Then the next thing you know, we're being overrun with the little bastards. They swarmed in like some sort of biblical plague or something."

Rustay grunted a nod. Leaning forward, he placed the tip of the cigar in the offered flame and puffed. The spicy-sweet scent of tobacco replaced the soothing scent of the region's lavender industry.

"That's about what it looked like with the column of German armor we came across a few miles back. Something had shredded a group of Panzer tanks like they were tissue paper."

I followed Rustay's gaze as he looked at something on the ground behind me. Impaled on the wrench I'd used to kill the first creature were three more of the things

"You wouldn't think it to look at them, but my guess is these guys hit that column first before they found your airfield."

"What do you think they are?"

"No idea, but besides reporting on the failure of our original missions, we need to get this to someone so they can run it up the chain." He let out a long, reluctant sigh. "Grabowski!"

"Yes, sir?"

"You, Hollywood, and Doyle go ahead and police the bodies. Use the fieldstones from that wall over there to cover them."

"Dammit," Hollywood grumbled.

"Sure. We'll get right on it," Grabowski said.

Rustay turned back to me, his face obscured in a cloud of thick smoke.

"Thanks," I said, meaning it. They were *my* guys.

"Don't mention it, Sergeant," he said to me with a nod. "It'll at least keep the vultures off the poor bastards." He puffed on the cigar again. "I want you to bag and tag those critters you killed over there, then gather your gear and get to work with Pierce. I want to be in the air before it gets dark."

"You don't have to tell me twice," I said. "I'd much rather not be here if those things decide to come back."

After a brief search, I was able to find my revolver and my rucksack in what remained of the small barn. The night before was still a blur in my mind. I gathered up my things and prepped *Jumpin' Jess* for flight with a little help from the jarhead, Pierce. The things had gouged holes through a few of the aircraft's sheet metal panels. We were lucky nothing structural had been damaged in the attack. After swapping a few hydraulic lines from one of the other aircraft and splicing two fairly large wire bundles back together, we loaded up.

The P-61 Black Widow was one hell of an armored beast. The original design for the aircraft had been based on the contract requirements of the British Purchasing Commission for a night fighter, which included the use of the newly developed Airborne Intercept radar, or AI for sort, which was a self-contained unit capable of being installed on a smaller aircraft. This contract was driven by Britain's urgent need for a high altitude, high-speed night flyer to intercept the Luftwaffe bombers attacking London. Jack Northrop's vision included a dual engine, dual tail boom design with a three-man crew of pilot, gunner, and radar operator, equipped with forward search radar, tail warning radar, four 20mm Hispano AN/M2 cannons, four .50 caliber M2 Browning machine guns, and the capability to carry either bombs or unguided rockets on its wing mounts made it one hell of a heavy fighter.

Warrant Officer Pierce, being the only pilot among our battered and pieced together crew, sat in the pilot's seat. I strapped into the gunner's position just above and behind the pilot, while the rest of the Joes stuffed themselves into the radar operator's compartment at the rear of the crew compartment. There wasn't anything comfortable about it, but we were all aboard. Powering

Widowmakers

Jess to full throttle, we rolled across the empty field and quickly took to the sky. I looked out of the gunner's window and watched as the ground gradually dropped away. Pierce banked the plane to the left, steering us to the northwest in the direction of the Omaha Beach HQ.

Chapter 3

After a short flight over the beautiful countryside of northern France, we arrived at Omaha Beach HQ, and were directed to park at the end of the airfield. Staff Sergeant Rustay had gotten on the horn while in transit and radioed our situation ahead to HQ. Since we were the only ones wearing headsets, Pierce and I could easily hear the confusion in the soldier's voice on the opposite end of the radio when he repeated Rustay's words back to us. Two jeeps packed full of armed Military Police jumped and bounced down the field in our direction as Pierce brought *Jumpin' Jess* to a full stop and chopped her throttles. The MPs piled out of the jeeps and surrounded the plane, weapons drawn. We cautiously opened the boarding hatches and climbed out one by one with our hands raised in the air.

"Which one of you would be Staff Sergeant Rustay?" The NCO in charge of the MP's stepped forward, a Thompson cradled over his left arm.

"That would be me," Rustay said, ducking low as he crossed under the number two engine nacelle.

"Bring the evidence and come with us."

I tossed the sack containing the two intact creature corpses to Rustay. Without question, he climbed into the

Jeep with the MP sergeant, who drove them away into the heart of the HQ camp. The second Jeep and all three of its occupants remained behind watching us, their weapons at the ready.

Out of habit, I began my post-flight walk around and noticed how soft the ground felt here and how *Jess's* tires had pushed the turf ahead of them.

"Couldn't you have found a better place to park, Pierce? We're gonna sink if we leave her here for too much longer."

"Hey, I did like they said and put her at the end of the field," Pierce argued.

I turned and looked at the guards. "Hey, do you guys have a tractor or a tug of some kind that we can use? We gotta get her moved to more solid ground." I thumbed behind myself toward the aircraft as I stepped around the propellers and approached them.

The three remaining guards responded by bringing their weapons to bear on me. "You'll stay where you are until we get the all-clear on you guys."

"Hey, pal, we're on the same side here," Hollywood said nervously. "What gives?"

"For all we know, you're all German spies. When the colonel gives the all clear, you can do whatever you need to do. Until then, you'll stay where you are, or we'll plug you full of holes." The guard hungrily licked his lips in that psychopathic way, like he hadn't had the chance to kill anyone since before breakfast.

"Make yourselves comfortable," the MP said. He reached over into the back of the Jeep and began tossing cans of C-rations in our direction.

Pierce caught the first of the cans and turned it around, looking at the label. "Aw, come on guys. You couldn't cut us a break and toss us an M-unit? There's only so many B-units I can take."

"You'll take what you're given or nothing at all," the lead MP said in a snarky tone. "Get comfortable and don't give me any trouble, and I won't have to put you out of my misery. Capisce?"

"I could eat the rancid ass end of a donkey at this point," Grabowski said as he picked up a can from the ground. "I don't care if it's meat or not as long as it's something in my stomach."

Each of us picked up one of the offered cans of rations and took a seat under *Jess's* wing, munching on the dry, cracker-like biscuits and candy pieces. Most ate quietly with one wary eye on the anxious MP. In the little bit of conversation we did have, I'd learned that Staff Sergeant Craig Rustay, Private First Class Richard 'Hollywood' Smith, Corporal Leonard Grabowski, and Private Kenneth Doyle had all been part of an infiltration team with the 325th Glider Infantry Regiment. Their mission had been to infiltrate and disrupt the Nazi supply depot on the outskirts of Chartres, southwest of Paris, in hopes it would weaken the effectiveness of the German tank divisions operating in the area. Shortly after takeoff, the latching mechanism that connected their glider to the C-47 Skytrain by way of a tow cable malfunctioned and released the team miles before their intended target area.

With little visibility and no landmarks to guide them across this area of the darkened countryside, the pilot set the craft down in a mostly flat field of wheat. The glider flipped and tore itself apart upon impact with the stone wall at the end of the field, and tumbled down an embankment, coming to rest partially submerged in the L'Eure river. Of their thirteen-man team, only the four of them had survived the crash. They found themselves behind enemy lines north of the village of Falaise.

After the crash, Rustay and the other survivors took inventory of their supplies and equipment, but were unable to find the high explosives that were essential to their mission to destroy the supply depot. Rustay assumed the explosives had been lost to the rain-swollen river with the forward section of the glider—and the pilot, whose body they never found. Together they'd made the decision to retreat back to friendly territory for reassignment while wreaking as much havoc on the enemy as possible. In the process of their trek across the French countryside, they'd stumbled across Lance Corporal Sheamus O'Brian of the British Corps of Royal Engineers, 42nd Assault Regiment, 1st Assault Brigade, and Warrant Officer James Johnson Pierce of the United States Marine Corps, whose Curtis Seahawk scout aircraft had been shot out of the sky by enemy anti-aircraft fire during a routine recon mission.

O'Brian took a swig from his canteen and passed it to me. "'Tis good for what ails ya, lad. Take a sup and pass it along," he said with a wink.

Happily I took the offered sip, letting the warm, earthy liquid slide slowly down my throat. It was a well-aged whiskey, with a bold but not overpowering flavor. It was smooth and had a faint spicy flavor. I passed the canteen to Private Doyle on my right.

"But I don't drink," Doyle said.

"Laddy?" O'Brian said in a questioning tone. He leaned forward to glare at Doyle. "Does your mother know you're a bloody blasphemer? I should wash your filthy mouth out with soap for a comment like that."

"I've just never cared for the taste of it," Doyle defended himself.

O'Brian let out an angry hiss. "If for no other reason, lad, do it for the family name," O'Brian goaded him.

In that next moment, I was emotionally torn for the private. I wasn't sure if I should be proud of him, or if I should feel sorry for him. He held up the flask in salute and took a deep breath.

"For the family," he said, then turning up the canteen, gulped down a full swallow of whiskey. "Oh! Jesus hates me!" He began to cough uncontrollably.

"I don't think that's the case, lad, but sure as tomorrow, you'll be hating yourself later." O'Brian chuckled.

"It can't be any worse than some of the cheap gin that's passed around at those ritzy parties as top shelf," Hollywood said as he reached for the canteen and took a swig himself. He let out a breath, smacking his lips. "That isn't bad at all." He passed the canteen to Grabowski.

The MPs turned, looking back at the sound of an approaching Jeep. I stood, dusting grass off my pants, and quickly spotted Staff Sergeant Rustay sitting in the passenger seat of the Jeep as it skidded to a stop on the damp grass.

"The Sarge is back," Private Doyle said, then let out a quiet hiccupped burp.

The others stood and began to gather around.

"What's the word?" Pierce said.

Staff Sergeant Rustay glared awkwardly at each of us, his gaze stern and tight-lipped. He turned back to the MPs and spoke in a commanding tone, "I think we can handle things from here, fellas." He smiled and nodded at them with one of those *you can leave any time* sort of looks.

The MP NCO pointed toward the middle of the field base. "Three rows over, and you'll find the chow hall. Two rows behind that you'll find the latrines, and the main supply tent is back over by command, where we just were."

"The heads up is appreciated, Sergeant…," Rustay said in a questioning tone.

"Beckwith. Staff Sergeant J.D. Beckwith," the MP NCO said.

"It's appreciated, Sergeant Beckwith," Rustay said, extending his hand.

"Just doing our jobs," he said as they shook, then looked over at his men. "These guys are under Archer's jurisdiction. You'd better be damned sure they're in the wrong before you give them any trouble. Now load up." Beckwith climbed back into the vehicle and turned over the Go-Devil engine of the Willys Jeep. He nodded at Rustay, then pulling a tight U-turn, raced along the airfield. Rustay watched the two Jeeps and their occupants retreat into the distance.

Hollywood approached the captain and quietly cleared his throat. "What was that all about, Sarge?"

Rustay snapped his head around to face Hollywood and the others. He took a deep breath and let out a long sigh as he fidgeted with something in his right palm. "We've been tasked with an important, if a bit unorthodox, mission. Our new designation is Whiskey Mike squad. We've been placed under the command of a brand new first lieutenant from the Army and will report all actions and findings directly to Marine Colonel Archer. This also includes the both of you," Rustay said, pointing at the Irishman and the Marine. "Pierce, you'll remain with us instead of returning to the USS *Arkansas*. We're in need of a pilot, and there aren't any others to spare, not to mention your specialization in recon could prove invaluable. O'Brian, because of your passion and talent for turning large things into smaller things, you're on indefinite loan from His Majesty's Army until your services are no longer required."

"Wait, what?" Pierce scratched his head. "How can they do that?"

"Caoineadh fuilteacha," O'Brian said, then spit to the side.

"Because apparently Task Force 13 gets preference," Rustay said.

"What the hell," Hollywood complained. "What did we do to get stuck working for a fucking jarhead?" Hollywood quickly threw up an apologetic hand in Pierce's direction. "Present company excepted, of course."

Pierce shot him a glance of burning anger.

"Yeah, this doesn't sound like it's going to be good, Sarge," Grabowski said.

Doyle stepped closer, nervously picking at his thumbnail. "What sort of mission is it?"

"Probably a suicide mission," O'Brian grumbled under his breath in his deep Irish brogue. "The luck, she has left me to be sure."

"So how the hell does this work? I didn't sign up to be a Marine," Hollywood said. "Are they going to try and cut our pay along with our IQs?" He laughed, then punched Pierce in the shoulder. "Oh, shit, um… Sorry about that...um...sir."

Pierce quietly smoldered, still glaring at Private Hollywood.

"We're all still part of our respective branches of service, with the rank and pay entitled to each of us as such. The only difference is we'll be taking direct orders from Col. Archer, and our pay will be coming from Task Force 13's coffers. Otherwise, a mission is a mission, and we'll strive to succeed in all we do! Do I make myself clear?" He barked the question, then glared at Hollywood and O'Brian.

"Hooah!" I said loud and clear from the back of the group. The others chimed in with their own shouts, even if they were somewhat reluctant and unenthusiastic.

"Our first order of business is to establish our squad outpost and requisition supplies. Since we've seen what those things can do first hand, they'll become our primary focus after we get set up. Once we're operational, we're to hunt down and exterminate the threat those creatures pose to our forces on the ground, by any means necessary. That's where you'll really come in handy, Pierce. You'll be our eye in the sky, and our air support as we move in and mop up an area. We'll be supplied with ammo, fuel, and rations on request, but we're on our own for any major aircraft parts for the moment."

"Well, hell," I interrupted. "Give me half a day, and we'll have plenty of parts. We can go back to the airfield and strip those planes for everything they're worth, if the

LT will allow it. The more hands we have, the better, but I'd really only need two or three guys, a few trucks, and a crane or winch on one of them to lift the heavier parts, like engines."

"I'll see what I can do about that when we're done here," Rustay said. "O'Brian, Doyle, and Hollywood, you'll be with Sullivan on this."

O'Brian cleared his throat. "So, what about this first looey they're sending us to break in? Is he the useful and capable type, or is he the sit around on your arse reading reports and drinking coffee all day type?"

"The paddy has a point," Hollywood said with a sideways nod.

"Pogue mo thoin," O'Brian growled, then spit on Hollywood's boot.

"Cool your heels! Both of you!" Rustay scowled at the two men, then straightened and let out a long breath. "To answer your question, I'd say he's the useful and capable type, but that's just my own personal opinion." Rustay held out a closed fist toward Pierce. "Even though you're a Marine, you're still the highest-ranking member of the team."

Pierce glanced up at Rustay, then curiously looked back to the offered hand.

"Hold out your hand," Rustay said.

"Why am I suddenly having flashbacks of my older brother?" Pierce reluctantly held out his hand palm up and cringed when Rustay opened his fist, dropping two black bars into his open palm.

"You've got to be shitting me!" Doyle let out a chuckle.

"Nope," Rustay said, then turned back to Pierce. "Would you please pin those on me?"

"The next thing you know, we're gonna find you with your nose buried up the colonel's ass," Hollywood said, snorting.

Nearly everyone burst out laughing at that comment. Granted it was a bit funny considering the situation, but it still irked me to no end.

I smacked Hollywood across the chest with the back of my hand. "Better watch it, *Hollywood.* He's an officer now."

Pierce's eyes narrowed as he looked down at his chest, then over to me. He smoothed back the wave of his thick black hair. "What's it to you?"

"Show some respect," I said, then nodded back toward the LT.

"Pierce," Rustay said.

"Oh! Yeah, sure thing, Lieutenant Rustay." Pierce smiled. He firmly gripped the staff sergeant stripes on either of Rustay's sleeves and tore them away with one good yank. He handed the stripes back to the LT and removed the backs of the pins. After placing them on the collar of Rustay's uniform, he firmly slapped a hand down on each of the pins. "Congratulations, *sir!*" He saluted Rustay with a shit-eating grin.

"Officer on deck!" I said with a chuckle, then popped a firm salute in Rustay's direction. The others, including Hollywood, followed my lead. They chuckled under their breath, and we fell in line as if we were about to be inspected. Even O'Brian and Pierce jumped into line with the rest of us.

"Oh, ha, ha, ha," Rustay said, scowling at the lot of us. He popped to attention and returned a sharp salute. "Now will you bunch of apes cut it out? We've got work to do."

"Sure, thing there, *LT*," Hollywood said. "So who's doing what?"

"I need a staff sergeant," Rustay said, holding out the pair of stripes in his hand. "Sullivan, you up for the job?"

I stood there dumbfounded. "You just met me and you want me as your staff sergeant?"

"Well, I assume you're capable of doing the job, since you've already made the rank of sergeant. Plus, I have no experience with airfield operations. I need someone to run the day to day operations for the aircraft, and I'd prefer if you were in charge of that instead of me."

"Hey," Pierce said. "So, what am I now? Chopped liver?"

Rustay turned back to Pierce with a mischievous smile. "Not at all. Since you're our only pilot, you'll either be in the air or getting your crew rest. No arguments," he said with a daring glare. He turned back to me and smiled. "So, do you want the job?"

"I have no doubt I can do the job, LT," I said. "If it's going to be nothing but paperwork and dishing out orders, I'll pass. If I still get to turn wrenches and keep the bird in the air, sure. I'll take the job."

"You'd better keep turning wrenches," Rustay said. "You're the only mechanic we have at the moment."

"Then we have a deal," I said and took the offered stripes.

"Grabowski!"

"Yeah, Sarge…I mean, sir, er…LT," Grabowski said, stuttering. We all laughed at his fumbling around.

"I need a sergeant as well. Think you're up to the job?"

"Sure, LT." Grabowski's goiter bobbed oddly as he nervously swallowed.

"Pass off your stripes once you get yours swapped out, Sullivan."

"Will do, LT."

"Of course you pass over the Irishman. Bloody fucking yanks." O'Brian spit out a thick wad of chewing tobacco.

"Of *course* he did," Hollywood said. "No one cares about a damn dirty spud eater."

"Shut it, Hollywood," Rustay ordered. "I haven't forgotten about you, O'Brian." He flashed a mischievous smile at the Irishman. "Trust me, I have an idea. Have you ever made napalm or something similar?"

"Oh, um, aye. Aye, I have. More than a time or two, to be sure." O'Brian winked.

"Good," Rustay said, then turned to me. "Sullivan. Is there any way to rig up the aircraft to carry bombs of any kind?"

"Yeah, LT," I said. "There's a mount point on each wing that can be used for bombs, missiles, or external fuel tanks. It just depends on the mission for how she gets loaded out."

"Good," Rustay said. "O'Brian. I want you to get me a list of the supplies you'll need to build us some bombs we can strap to the plane…"

"*Jess*," I said, interrupting.

Rustay turned back to me with a confused look.

"Her name is *Jumpin' Jess* or *Jess*," I said.

"Alright." Rustay let out a little laugh. "I want to load *Jess* with a surprise gift for those creatures."

"Was there any word about those wee beasties when you went to command? We can't be the only ones to have encountered the bloody fae folk."

"O'Brian's right," I said. "You'd think someone else would have seen something by now. Did they have any info on those things?"

"They didn't have much more info to give. Other teams have run into destroyed German equipment similar to what we've seen, but there haven't been any more reports from allied forces."

"That's 'cause they all know better," Hollywood said. "They'd get shipped off in a straitjacket if they started talking about boogie men."

"Even so," Rustay said. "Colonel Archer made us point on these creatures since we've had the most experience with them. There's a rumor floating around that they were created by the Nazis to attack the allied forces."

"They must be pretty desperate or lacking in manpower if they're sending things like that against us," Pierce said.

"But we've already seen what they did to that line of Panzers we found," Doyle said.

"Exactly, which is why I'd dismiss the rumor of a secret Nazi weapon. The colonel thinks they're either an undocumented animal of some sort, which we know is possible, or they're possibly something from myth that has only ever been rarely seen."

"Well if that's the case," Grabowski said, "what the hell has them stirred up, and in these kinds of numbers?"

"Oh, I don't know, Ski," Hollywood said sarcastically. "How about another great war fought on their turf?"

"The colonel did mention one thing," Rustay said. "Marching troops haven't had a run in with these things yet. Only mechanized convoys, trucks, tanks, that sort of thing have been hit. There was one report he mentioned where a unit found a train and its cars in pieces. The report specified that it looked ripped and torn apart, and not by explosives."

"And airfields," I added.

"And airfields," Rustay corrected. "Let's hit the chow hall before anything else. Grabowski, you and Hollywood see about getting a tent and gear to set up shop. I'll find us a place to call home. The rest of you know what to do after you eat?"

Everyone nodded

"Good, then let's go. I'm starving. Even mystery meat sounds good right about now."

Chapter 4

After a five-star meal fit for any Army grunt in the finest dining facility this side of the Seine river, we spent the rest of the evening setting up what looked like a campaign tent left over from the Great War at the end of the runway. Pierce fired up *Jess* and moved her nearer to our new unit location. I was the first one up the next morning. Careful not to wake anyone else, I grabbed my canteen and pack, and went outside to stir the fire and brew myself a cup of coffee. Doyle had scrounged up a few rocks from nearby to use as a fire ring, and Grabowski, being the aspiring chef he is, had managed to wrangle up a pot, a skillet, and a few cooking utensils.

In shortly under an hour, Grabowski had managed to whip up some of the best-damned omelets I've ever tasted in my life. He'd managed to acquire the eggs from an undisclosed location, mixed in some finely chopped bits of hard salami he'd picked up from an abandoned farmhouse, and a good helping of wild onions that he liberally sprinkled into the mix for good measure. It wasn't much, but even the small bites each of us had were enough to improve morale by enough to make the evening nearly enjoyable. Though passing around O'Brian's canteen surely didn't hurt anything, either.

Grabowski told us about his lifelong desire to become a famous chef and to serve dignitaries and heads of state at the White House. His parents, being the practical kind of folks they were, repeated the same answer time and again. *Pull your head out of the clouds, boy. Daydreams don't put food on the table, and one day you'll have a family of your own to feed and raise,* they'd told him. And they'd done just that.

His family was originally from Kenosha, Wisconsin, and had moved to North 36th street in Milwaukee in 1934 during the brewery boom after the end of Prohibition. His dad, Fred, got a job working the vats for Banner Brewing Company, and his mom, Lavern, worked in the main office for the Miller Brewing Company. Lenny had more or less raised himself on the streets of Milwaukee, since his parents worked from before dawn until after sunset. Being the youngest of seven, he was left in the care of his older siblings, who were home about as much as their parents. Eventually, Lenny managed to land a job doing flunky work at the Harley Davidson factory, sweeping floors and cleaning parts, before being drafted into the Army.

I'm sure glad my paw was never like that. He wanted all seven of us to become something better than the cotton farming sharecropper from the Chattanooga valley he'd become. He always use to tell me, "If you can think it, it's gotta be possible. If you can see it, it's an attainable goal. You just have to figure out how to get there from here, just like navigating the side of a mountain to get the deer you'd shot and now had to carry out of the woods."

Well, that right there is one reason I'd moved up to Chattanooga and went out on my own before the Army snatched me up. I tried out a number of jobs around town, working in the Read House as a bell boy, to moving cargo on the docks down at the river, to working in the foundry on the south side of Saint Elmo, and even a short stint as a draftsman with Sherman and Reilly over at Ross's Landing. One of their engineers had noticed me scribbling one day while eating my lunch down at the docks and asked if I'd like to give it a shot. They had me drawing sheaves and parts for winches or cranes that needed to be forged or fabricated. And that's about the time the letter came from the Army.

Then there was PFC Richard "Hollywood" Smith. Wavy black hair, manicured, pencil-thin Clark Gable mustache, and icy blue eyes that could hypnotize a nun. But I tell you what, he was as mean and spiteful as a copperhead in the heat of summer. I honestly don't think he's ever liked another human being in his life. This guy was a real piece of work. I swear he must be part Nazi under that pretty boy exterior. It didn't matter who he was talking about, he always talked down to them, or berated them if he could. I don't know if it was to make himself feel better, or what, but his hillbilly jokes were starting to get old, and I could tell he was wearing on Lenny and O'Brian, too.

A self-proclaimed lady's man, he'd been raised in Hollywood, California his whole life, and his dream was to make it onto the big screen and see his name in lights. He'd worked in a number of hotels and restaurants around town when he finally caught a break and got a gig working on the sets of some of the most famous movies in Hollywood. Even though he was part of the lower end of contributing to the film, he'd still be part of movie greats like *Mr. Smith goes to Washington, Seven Sinners, The Wizard of Oz,* and *Gone with the Wind.* His one true claim to fame was being in a movie alongside the Hollywood elite, Gretta Garbo. He played the part of the busboy in the background of a hotel scene in *Two-Faced Woman* in '41.

Then there was Warrant Officer 'J.J.' Pierce. All in all, he really hadn't led an exciting or remarkable life. He'd told us the night before that the highlight of his year was when he could go back to work at one of the textile mills in Pensacola instead of working his father's fishing boat during the busy season. He was an only child growing up, had two dogs and a cat, and loved his mother's key lime pie.

By the time we'd gotten around the fire to Private Kenneth Doyle, he was already slurring his words and hanging on the Irishman's shoulder. He professed his love for photography, along with his love for all of us. He then proceeded to thank each and every one of us for being here with him to fight against the great evil of the Nazi Empire and its hordes of goblins, and promptly fell backwards off of the crate he'd been using as a seat, and began to snore.

O'Brian had been tight-lipped the entire night, even with Hollywood's persistent antagonizing. After a few hours of random banter and bullshit around the small campfire, he'd finally opened up a bit. He came from a long line of Celtic warriors and mercenaries, and thought this war was no different from any other that had come before or would come in the future. Members of his family had fought in every major conflict in Europe since the time of Joan of Arc, when they served as sappers alongside the Maid of Orleans herself during the Hundred Years War.

Then there was Lieutenant Craig Rustay. A native of Buffalo New York, he'd lived a fairly quiet and comfortable life compared to the rest of us. He was an All-Star starting quarterback and captain of the football team in his high school. He was the envy of his classmates, and sported the titles of Debate Team president, captain of the Chess Team, Key Club president, captain of his school's Civil Defense Club, and last but not least, he was the school's student body president.

His hours at home were usually spent alone in his room with his nose buried in a book, or down in the basement performing a new experiment to test a hypothesis. This was mainly because of the long hours that his father worked. His father, Douglas, worked as the senior chemist at a local military research lab, and the work schedule was driven by the military and the obligations of the contracts. When his father was home, he was either working in his home office, or entertaining military leaders and business clients.

His mother, Krista, would plan and prepare for these meetings with the whip crack haste of a nun with a ruler. Regularly his father would call home in the late afternoon and inform her that he would be bringing a client home for dinner. She would then proceed to send their housekeeper to the store for the needed supplies, while she laid out a fresh new tweed jacket for his father before she freshened herself up with a newly pressed dress, her finest pearls, and a reapplied layer of cherry red lipstick.

After high school he applied to the Army, fast burned his way through any training he could take, and graduated with honors, finding himself assigned to the 82nd Airborne Division.

For a mostly thrown together unit, we seemed to mesh well together—or at least we did while telling tales around the campfire. After gathering a bit of firewood from the nearby stand of trees, I stirred the coals and had a nice, steady flame burning in the fire ring. After adding water and the small brown cube of condensed instant coffee from the ration packs to the cup portion of my canteen, I placed it on a flat stone within the fire ring.

While I waited for the small flame to warm the drink enough for it to properly steep, I moseyed my way over to *Jess*. She was midnight black from tip to tail, with thin red lines that highlighted her airframe and her wings. I passed my hand over the skin of her nose, inspecting the rivets around where the nose art had been painted. "Suppose I should scrounge up some paint and add a unit insignia to you," I said quietly to the plane as I appreciated the lines and curves of her design. "Whiskey Mike squad," I said, rolling the name around on my tongue. "Whiskey Mike, W M." I paused, looking up at the image of *Jess*. "You're a Black Widow. Whatcha think about Widowmakers?" I patted her on the side of the fuselage.

"Mind if I join you?

I spun around to find Lieutenant Rustay cutting a path across the dew-covered field. "Not at all, LT. It's a free country…or at least it will be when we're done. I was just giving *Jess* a little preflight while my coffee warmed up."

"I saw," he said. "I set mine up as well before coming over. She seems like a fine piece of machinery. Heavily armed and armored, if I'm not mistaken?"

"Yes sir, she is. She was designed to sneak up and cut a German aircraft out of the sky under the cover of night."

"What are her downsides?"

"In all truth, LT, she's a bit of a heavy girl. See those C-47 Skytrains?" I pointed at a group of cargo aircraft lined up on the opposite side of the runway. "They can weigh up to 31,000 pounds on takeoff. Our girl here, fully loaded, can easily be closer to 40,000 pounds. It doesn't sound like much, but it makes a difference. See how she's already sinking in the ground here?"

"Yeah, that's not a good thing, is it?"

"No sir, it's not. This field may be good for those transports, but we'd be more suited to an airfield designed for bombers, or like the one we were at previously. Pastureland, not farmland. The ground is more solid and compacted."

"What can you do to reduce her weight?"

I scratched at the back of my head and looked her over from one end to the other. "In all reality, I could maybe take out some of the armor plating around the crew compartment, but there really isn't anything else I can take off of her. Why?"

"I've just been thinking of possible options to her loadout, depending on what we recover from the airfield we found you at. Possibly add a few more guns to her, or some extra bomb mounts to expand our capabilities."

"With a little elbow grease, yeah, probably. Anything's possible as long as you can dream it, LT."

He smiled at me. I could see his mind working over the possibilities of that phrase.

"Okay, good," he said, snapping out of his inner thoughts. "Those trucks I requested should be here in an hour or two. Oh, and I arranged for a few extra mechanics to go with us and Pierce. I want him getting dirty. He needs to know this plane inside and out, just in case he runs into any issues while out on a mission."

"I am certified to run the radar and the turret."

"That may be so, but you won't always be on board to help, either. There may be times you'll be busy fixing other aircraft."

"Other aircraft?"

"Yep," he said with a smirk. "That's the plan, at least."

"Oh," I said. Moving to the side, I pointed at the 2nd Pursuit Squadron insignia on the side of the aircraft. "I was thinking of changing the unit patch, sir."

"What did you have in mind?"

"Well, Whiskey Mike squad doesn't exactly roll off the tongue well. I was considering Widowmakers instead, since she is a Black Widow."

"I love it," Rustay said. "I have faith in you, Sullivan. Come up with whatever you want for a mascot, and put it on the plane."

I smiled. "Widowmakers it is then."

"Good, now let's get back over to the fire. That coffee should be ready by now," he said and slapped me on the shoulder.

We all went about our morning routine, then hit the chow hall before things got crowded. I hurried, shoving a plate of fried potatoes and a bowl of grits down my throat, then headed over to supply to see what I could wrangle for paint. After a bit of discussion and even more bartering, I was able to score a few small tins of paint and rushed back to the airfield.

Since I didn't have any sandpaper, I used my pocketknife to rough up the surface of the existing unit patch, ruining the image of the dapper dressed beagle, then carefully painted over the area with a base coat of white. By the time Lieutenant Rustay and the others returned, I'd finished the unit patch, and was putting the finishing strokes of 'WO Pierce' on the side of the aircraft, just under the side of the pilot's window. All in all, it wasn't too bad. Two coats of white, a simple black border with a black circle, and a red hourglass shape in the center of that. In small white and shadowed lettering at the top of the patch was 'Whiskey Mike Squad', and below in larger, bolder letters that caressed the lower section of the patch was 'Widowmakers'.

"Well now, looks like you've been busy," Pierce said as he approached from the squad tent. He looked upward toward the cockpit and smiled, admiring my work. "You did that?"

"Yup," I said and smiled back. "Figured it was only right, since she's going to be yours to fly."

"You'd better add your name to the other side."

"Why's that?"

"For one, she was your girl first," he said, draping his arm over my shoulders. "For two, you're the dedicated crew chief on her. That at least entitles you to some privileges."

"Alright then," I said and moved the ladder I'd borrowed from another unit in camp.

"Rustay sent me over here to get you. The trucks will be here any minute, so finish that up and get ready to go."

"Will do," I said as I snatched the paint can and climbed the rickety wooden ladder.

Widowmakers

Chapter 5

We set out that morning with three trucks and a handful of tools I was able to scrounge up. Pierce, Doyle, O'Brian, Lieutenant Rustay, and two guys from motor pool to help drive and turn wrenches loaded up their packs and a weeks' worth of rations for the lot of us. Once we'd gotten on the road on our way back to Air Base Jackson, the LT told me that at first, the motor pool guys were only going to give him one truck. He tossed around Archer's name and promised the guy a bottle of good scotch he'd been saving for a special occasion. He confessed that he'd really wanted to save that bottle to toast the guys he'd lost in the crash. It was the bottle he'd brought with him to celebrate when they accomplished their mission. But now he had an entirely new mission, and a new team that was counting on him to come through. So, his selfless deed benefited us with extra trucks and a few extra able bodies.

We traveled for most of the day down backcountry roads that reminded me of the rolling hills of Northwest Georgia. Sometime in the late afternoon, we came across the group of German tanks they'd previously found, which had led to them finding me and the airfield. The tanks were destroyed. There weren't any holes or signs of explosives, but the steel had been torn, and looked as if it had been chewed on in places.

The LT leapt from the passenger seat of the lead truck as it slowed and stopped alongside the devastation.

"Doesn't look any different this time than it did before," Pierce said, leaning over in my direction.

"Let's see if there's anything useful we can recover from here," Rustay said as he knelt to inspect a piece of shredded metal plate. He fingered the three deep gouges in the surface of the metal.

"Lieutenant," O'Brian said as he climbed onto the turret of the lead tank. "If any of those Kraut shells are still intact, would we have room for them in the trucks? I could use the powder from them for a few special projects, if that be alright with you, sir."

"I think we'd be alright with that," Rustay said, then crossed his arms and thought for a moment. "Actually, strike that, O'Brian. You and you," he said, pointing at the two drivers, "load all the shells, and siphon the fuel from the tanks. We can dump some of the rounds if we need the space for aircraft parts once we get to the airfield."

O'Brian grinned wide, then disappeared into the top of the Panzer. Maniacal laughter reverberated from the steel enclosure. "That's right, me pretties. You all get to go home with me, where I promise you, you will not be displeased with what I have in store for you."

Rustay cupped his hands around his mouth and shouted, "O'Brian!"

The bowler hat and copper-topped Irishman appeared from the top hatch of the Panzer. "Oh, aye, Lieutenant? I was just about to start moving these shells."

"Don't worry about that. The drivers and Doyle can handle it," Rustay said, then turned to Pierce. "You and Sullivan and me will set up camp here for the night. I want you to backtrack that trail and see if you can figure out where those things came from. We already know where they went, but if we can see where they came from, we might learn something new about them."

"Oh, aye. Those wee beasties left a trail wide enough that a blind man could see."

"Grab your gear and head out," Rustay said as he started to walk away, then stopped and turned back. "Here, take this with you." He unslung his Thompson and handed it up to O'Brian, who hung out the hatchway.

"To be sure, Lieutenant, you'd not want to keep the rifle for yourself?"

"No. I'll be fine with my sidearm, O'Brian. You take it just in case you need it. There're two more clips in the side of my pack in the lead truck. Snag those before you head out."

"Aye, sir," O'Brian said, saluting Rustay in a limp-wristed British salute.

O'Brian followed the trail to the north through the woods while we stripped the weapons and anything else that could be usable from the bodies of the German soldiers. Rations, ammo, even small personal effects that could be used in trade back at base were salvaged. At one point, Lieutenant Rustay threated one of the drivers with a court-martial for desecrating the corpses when he caught the guy trying to beat the gold teeth from the soldier's mouth.

Shortly after that had been dealt with, we set up a bucket brigade to move the shells from the tanks and loaded them into one of the trucks. Twenty-two of the seventy-five-millimeter rounds were neatly stacked in the back of one of our transports, along with three fully functional MG 34 machine guns, and all the 7.92mm ammunition we could find. After that, we set about further disabling the tanks in any way we could. From cutting hoses and electrical lines, to smashing valves, and anything else we could easily break, along with removing as much of the electrical harnesses from the engine bay as we could.

To be on the safe side, we muddled through cold rations, and took turns on watch through the night. Two men, two hours at a time, just to make sure no one fell asleep and we didn't get surprised by Germans or rabid jackrabbit things.

Just after dawn the next morning, O'Brian wandered out of the woods, looking cold and tired.

"Remind me to check my bloody batteries the next time I go wandering off in the woods." He tossed his flashlight at Doyle. "Be a good lad and change those out for me, if you wouldn't mind."

"Do it your damned self," Doyle said, tossing the flashlight back to O'Brian.

"I was starting to wonder if you might have found a cottage with an innocent farm girl or something," Pierce said.

"Hey, LT, O'Brian is back," Doyle said loudly.

"If only I were that lucky, lad." He laughed between the chattering of his teeth. "It gets a wee bit nippy out when the dew settles down on everything."

"What did you find?" Rustay asked as he approached. "Hey, you, what's your name, soldier?" he said, pointing at one of the drivers.

"Specialist Steven Perunko, sir," the driver said.

"Perunko, snag a ration for O'Brian here. I'm sure he's hungry by now."

"Yes, sir," he said and climbed into the back of one of the trucks.

The lieutenant continued over to where we were gathering around O'Brian, stepping between us. "What did you find?"

"I might have found an old nest or den, but now it just looks abandoned."

"Maybe they aren't coming back this way," Doyle said.

"Could be," Rustay said, "but what makes you think it's a den?"

"For one, it stunk to high heaven of the things. My nose may not be as good as a hound's nose, but I can smell the stench of those things as I sure as I can smell Hollywood's mother from across the room."

We all fought to hold back the laughter we were feeling on the inside, even the lieutenant. He smiled and took a deep breath, composing himself. "Besides the smell, what else was there?"

"The rest of the Germans we didn't find here. There wasn't really much of them left. Mostly torn and bloody uniforms, though I did manage to find a hand." O'Brian dropped his pack and turned; digging into it, he produced something wrapped in a bloody piece of cloth.

Pierce gagged and turned, running behind one of the trucks. His retching could easily be heard by anyone within a hundred yards.

Doyle watched, captivated, as O'Brian began to unwrap the object. "Is that what I think it is?"

"Hmm," O'Brian said, looking up at the private. "Oh, aye, lad. I was hoping Sullivan there had a pair of cutters I could use to get the fingers out of the rings on this hand," he said, nodding in my direction.

Rustay's eyes narrowed to a perturbed scowl.

"What?" O'Brian shrugged. "No sense in letting them go to waste. There's a good bit of gold and silver in them." He rewrapped the hand and tucked it back into his pack.

"Here's a thought," Rustay began, and he motioned for his Thompson. "Maybe that's exactly why we found all the bodies at the airfield."

O'Brian handed the heavy automatic rifle to the lieutenant. "If I have to, I suppose."

"The things were already full from their snack of Germans," Pierce said as he rounded the truck.

"Exactly." Rustay snapped his fingers. "But why did they demolish the aircraft?"

"Because they smelled funny?" Doyle suggested in a questioning tone.

"Maybe," Rustay said as he rubbed his chin in thought. "Either way, we still need to get to the airfield and strip it for everything it's worth. Let's take care of that, and maybe we can track down where they went to."

"You really should go look at the nest, sir. It's only a mile or so back in the forest. It just got too dark for me to see my hand in front of my face while I was out there. I climbed up in a tree and waited for daybreak. But truly, sir. You just need to go see it for yourself. It's too hard to describe to ya' proper enough."

We all started to disperse, when the LT piped back up, "O'Brian. Feel up to putting a few of those German shells to good use before we pull out?"

"Oh, absolutely, sir. It would be my pleasure. But what do you want me to do with them?"

"Permanently disable each of these tanks. Blow out their engines and turret tracks."

O'Brian's smile brightened the world at that moment. He licked his lips like a hungry wolf. "With pleasure, sir!"

"Sullivan and Doyle, you two are with me. Let's go take a look at this nest while O'Brian sets up the fireworks show."

I grabbed my rifle and pack, and waited by the blatantly obvious path the things had taken through the forest from the north, as Doyle and the LT did the same. We made short work of the mile-long hike. Each of us moved with stealthy purpose through the old-growth forest, while keeping a wary eye on our surroundings. Save for the obvious path through the forest, there was no other sign of the creatures, until we crested a small rise that dropped off steeply into a small ravine. The musky smell of the things wafted up on the lazy summer breeze that blew through the forest. Bits of uniforms, torn packs, and bloody bones that looked as if they'd been gnawed upon littered the bottom of the ravine. Careful of our footing on the wet leaves that covered the forest floor, we slid our way down the side of the ravine to find the entrance of a small cave.

"Yup, sure looks like a nest to me," Doyle said. "Are we done here? Can we go?"

"Not just yet," Rustay said as he crouched near the tattered remains of a German uniform.

I flipped open the top of a German rucksack that was torn down one side, its straps shredded like a cat had ran its back claws across them. I rummaged around inside the pack, pulling out a fairly new looking field coat, toiletries kit, a half-eaten ration package, and a nice-looking leather case wrapped in thick felt-like material. I opened the case and was surprised to find a very expensive German-made camera with an assortment of lenses. I closed up the case and rewrapped it in the cloth.

"Hey, Doyle!"

"Yeah, Sarge?"

"Didn't you say something about having a passion for photography?"

"It would be a dream come true if that was what my day job consisted of," Doyle said, patting his chest as he drifted off into the daydream.

"Well then, get started," I said, handing the bundle to the private.

"What's this?"

Rustay joined us, curiously looking at the wrapped item. "Find something?"

"Yeah, and something good for a change."

Doyle unwrapped the package and gasped, losing his ability to form words when he opened the case.

"Well, now, that is just gorgeous," Rustay said.

"Doyle was a professional photographer before the war," I said to the LT. "I think it would be a good idea to document everything we come across with these things."

"That's a good idea," Rustay agreed. "Remind me when we get back to base to put in a requisition for film, and anything else you'll need for processing it."

"You can count on it, Lieutenant." Doyle hugged the case. Rewrapping it in the thick material, he tucked it away in his own ruck.

"Ahem," I said, staring at the private. "You could start by documenting this area. Treat it like a crime scene. Get as many shots as you can from as many angles, and especially get pictures of any strange markings, or anything else these things may have left behind."

"I'll get right on it, Sarge," he said as he took up the camera and immediately began to take pictures.

"What do you think, LT?"

"I think O'Brian was right. There's no reason to bring body parts back here unless they were bringing it back to feed others. Like a pack of wolves or lions maybe. I just don't know," he said as he attempted to peer into the cave from a distance.

"I think I have all of the pictures I need here, LT," Doyle said as he poked at a bit of German uniform on the ground.

"Alright," Rustay said with a nod. "Unless you have something else, Sullivan, I'd say grab your gear and let's get back to the trucks.

"Just say the word."

"Then let's go," he said as he pulled a grenade from his pack and slung it back over his shoulders. "You two get back up to the top of the rise while I double-check for any survivors," he said with a grin as he pulled the pin on the grenade.

Chapter 6

By late evening, we'd arrived at the airfield—or at least what remained of the airfield. It was strangely silent. Everything was exactly as we'd left it a few days ago, and it suddenly hit me. I felt the flood of emotion well up and wash over me as I comprehended the loss of my men, my brothers, my friends…Tears poured down my face as I quietly sobbed to myself. I felt a gentle hand suddenly resting on my shoulder.

"What the bloody hell is wrong, lad?"

I turned to the Irishman, unsure of what to even say to a comment like that.

"This is a war, lad. Good people die for no other reason than they were in the wrong place at the wrong time. That's just how it is. You can either stand there weeping like a damned woman, or you can pull yourself together and make their lives count for something by getting on with our assignment."

He had a good point. Even if it was a bit of a cruel, cold-hearted point. I wiped the tears on my sleeves and sucked in a shaky breath.

O'Brian offered me his canteen with a sympathetic look. "It might not cure this particular ailment, but it'll at least help to take the edge off of it."

I took the canteen and tipped back a small swallow. "Thank you, O'Brian."

"You're welcome, lad. Trust me, I can sympathize with your pain," he said, then tipped back the canteen himself.

"When you're ready, Sullivan," Rustay said as he approached, unfolding a map. "Get the rest of the team to work on cannibalizing parts. O'Brian, I want you to follow the trail of those things and see where they might have gone to next." He studied the tree line around the field, then looked about to get his bearings. "We're roughly here aren't we, Sullivan?" he asked, pointing at the map.

"Yeah, I'd say that's pretty close."

"And if that's the direction they continued to go," he said, pointing with two fingers toward the east, "it's possible there may be more casualties in the village of Vieux."

"Would make sense to me," I said, looking up at the two of them.

"See what you can find out, O'Brian."

"Aye, sir," the Irishman said and saluted. Grabbing his pack and rifle, he trotted away in the direction of the path the creatures had left.

"Let's get to work, Sullivan," Rustay said, rolling up his sleeves. "Let's take everything that isn't nailed down, then we'll use a few more of those German shells to destroy what we can't carry away."

We busted our asses for the rest of the day, barely even stopping to eat. By the time we'd all had entirely enough fun for the day, we'd managed to salvage two engines, twelve M2 .50 caliber machine guns, two 20mm cannons from one, fuel, oils, more ammo than we could carry, and an assortment of other parts and pieces I'd had to replace regularly on other occasions. We overloaded the trucks and were ready to roll the next morning.

By pure accident, I'd come across a rosary while poking around in the remains of the barn for anything else of use. It was still attached to the severed hand of its owner. It hit me all of a sudden, I'd remembered seeing Russo cradle this very rosary as he said his evening prayers. Stepping on the pungent-smelling appendage, I wrapped my hand around the loose end of the rosary, and with a gentle tug, separated the two from one another. I fought back a tear as I examined the mahogany-colored beads. Even though Russo had been a major pain in the ass most of the time, he was still a good soldier, and an honest man.

O'Brian returned just before dark and said he'd found the remains of a village that had been burned to the ground in the direct path the creatures had taken through the forest. He'd searched the area around the village, but didn't find any other signs of the creatures, even in the next village over, so the burnt village could have just been a casualty of the war itself, and the creatures had only passed through.

I grabbed a ration from the truck and handed it to O'Brian as he dropped his pack and sat against the truck tire, pulling his boots off.

"Thank ya. That's a might kind of ya, laddy." He nodded and proceeded to remove his socks, laying them out across the top of his boots to air out.

"On more than one occasion I've seen you cross yourself like a Catholic," I said, "but I haven't seen you use a rosary yet. Do you have one with you?"

"No, lad. Unfortunately not. I don't know when exactly I lost it, but it was either after I was pushed out of that perfectly good airplane, or as I crashed through the top of a tree once I arrived in France." He flashed a wide, sarcastic smile. "Either way, it doesn't really matter. Gone is gone, so there's no need to make a fuss about it one way or another."

"Will this one do?" I held out the wooden rosary just in front of the Irishman. "It belonged to one of the men I lost here. I'm not a Catholic myself, but I'd rather see it used than buried or tucked away somewhere and forgotten. And considering what we're up against, you never can be too sure with things like this. I'd much rather see it put to good use." I could have sworn at that moment O'Brian's dry mutton chops became even bushier and full when he smiled.

He swelled with pride and nodded. "Aye, lad. That'll do, without a doubt." He beamed as he took the rosary from me and examined it closely. "That's good of you, son. God bless ya for having a kind heart." He nodded a smile and dug into the ration I'd handed him earlier.

The next morning we rolled out at a crawling pace, with the majority of us walking alongside the overloaded transports because of the lack of space. We made our way down a winding country road that brought us around a small hillock, and through the burned-out village O'Brian had come across in his search. It looked as if it had been destroyed some time ago. There was no fresh ash to be seen anywhere, only blackened and burnt remains of buildings. Charred bits of timbers stuck out at odd angles from the tops of the stone walls of the buildings that remained. We continued down the road for some time in search of signs of the creatures as we made a loop around the area.

"Smoke," Doyle said as he pointed off toward the northwest. Black smoke like from a tire fire roiled into the bright blue sky.

Rustay pulled out his trusty map as we walked alongside the lumbering trucks and looked about, examining our surroundings. "If I'm looking at this right, there should be another small village in that direction about two miles out."

"Do you suppose it would be the wee beasties, or the Germans, sir?"

"I don't know, but it won't hurt to be prepared for either one," Rustay said as he pulled the slide back on his Thompson and checked the breech. "Everyone get yourselves ready for a fight."

The *click, clack* of weapons checks resounded over the dreary hum of the big diesel engines. We continued at a slow trudge, rolling into the village just as the long shadows of late evening stretched across the fields. Smoke rose slowly skyward from the remains of two larger shops near the center of the small village.

"The wee devils 'ave been here, sir," O'Brian said, crossing himself. He wrapped the rosary around his right hand and pulled his rifle up to his shoulder, ready for anything.

"It sure looks like it," I said as I approached the still form of a child, who lay curled up on the ground. The remains were dressed in a bloody white dress with small buttercup flowers that polka-dotted the fabric. Trying to catch my breath, I choked and dryly swallowed. Fear raised the hair on the back on my neck.

Then a strange thing happened. At that moment, it was as if I could see the dark-haired little girl in her pretty white dress dancing about the village square. I could hear her soft-spoken words in French, her giddy laughter, and her squeals of excitement, which suddenly melded into screams of terror that echoed in the back of my mind as

I imagined what had happened to these poor people. I forced my eyes away from the small, helpless form.

Remains of innocent villagers and livestock littered the rest of the village square. There must have been a celebration of some sort going on the night before. Banners and ribbons stretched across the square and attached to the surrounding buildings. Thick garlands and wreaths of flowers decorated every building. A small stage had been erected to the side of the ornate stone fountain that occupied the center. Two shops that looked like something from the middle ages still burned and smoldered in places.

"Door to door," Rustay said shakily. "Let's see if we can find any survivors." It looked like he was struggling to fight back the same emotions I was.

"Y'all heard the LT, let's get on it! Doyle, to the right, O'Brian to the left," I ordered, then pointed toward an ancient stonework church that sat off to the side of the village. "Park the trucks over there and keep lookout. We don't want anyone sneaking up on us while we're otherwise occupied," I said to Perunko, the lead driver. He nodded and pulled his truck alongside the old church. The other two trucks followed suit, parking in line beside the first.

I admired the craftsmanship of the old church as I approached the ancient wooden doors of its entrance. Cautiously listening with my ear to the door, I unholstered my Army service revolver. Hearing nothing within, I pulled at the ornate iron door handle. The heavy wooden door swung open with little effort. Bright blues, reds, and yellows colored the sanctuary as the sun shone through the church's stained glass windows. It didn't look as if anything had happened here, but they had at least been here. I could smell the dank musky odor of the things in the stale air of the church. There was no sign of struggle or remains in sight, but then I heard the sickly wet gnawing of something behind one of the pews. Reminding myself to breathe, I quietly motioned for Perunko to follow, then continued slowly into the sanctuary. I moved like I was back home in the woods, stalking a deer. Each calculated step was slow and silent, like a panther creeping about the forest.

Quietly reaching the source of the noise, I craned my neck to get a better view, and froze. My stomach lurched as that little voice of reason in the back of my mind screamed for me to run. Ragged jackrabbit like ears flopped and jerked as the thing's blood-covered snout bobbed up and down. Leathery bat-like wings stretched outward as it tugged and strained against its meal. It tore at the large, meaty breast of its victim with a grotesque, bestial claw. Blood bubbled from around the thing's nostrils as it loudly lapped and slurped at the fatty yellow tissue. It tugged and ripped away a strip of flesh with a sickening, zipper-like popping. Fighting against my instinctual first reaction, my training took control. I took aim, pulled back the hammer, and fired. Black ichor sprayed from the creature's back. I pulled the hammer back and fired again, repeating another two times before the thing slumped to the ground, motionless.

"*Lieutenant!*" I heard Doyle shout, followed by a shrill, panic-laced cry.

I stepped forward and quickly checked the rest of the church, then turned and ran outside.

"Sullivan! Over here," Rustay shouted, waving me over as he ran toward a squat rectangular building just down the main street a little ways. Fumbling with the spent rounds in my revolver, I reloaded, then sprinted across the distance to catch up to the LT.

"Found one chewing on one of the villagers in the church," I said as I slid the revolver back into its holster.

"From his reaction," Rustay said, nodding at Doyle, "I'd say there may be a few in that building as well."

"Oh, there are. There's a whole nest of the things in there, sir!" Doyle leaned back against the door to the building, catching his breath. "They're hiding out in the tavern here," he said, thumbing at the building behind himself. He sucked in a long, ragged breath as he fought back panicked hyperventilation.

"How many? Ten, twenty, fifty?" Rustay asked.

Doyle's face contorted with disbelief. "The hell if I know! You really expect me to stop and count the things? I opened the door, saw them lying everywhere, one looked up at me like it had been sleeping, and I shut the door…sir," he said with a pleading afterthought look of apology.

Rustay shot a questioning glance in my direction, then turned back to Doyle. "Did you say they were lying about like they were sleeping?"

"Um…" Doyle stared off into space for a second, unsure what he'd just said. "Um…Yes! They were laying around like a pack of dogs snuggled up for the evening."

"Maybe we can eradicate these things here and now," Rustay said, turning back to me.

"Possibly." I shrugged. "Do you care about the building?"

"I'd rather not damage anything we don't have to, but considering the circumstances, I don't think any of the villagers will be complaining about it. Why?"

I looked back over my shoulder. "O'Brian!"

"Aye! What can I do for ya, Sarge?

"With what we have in the trucks, do you think you could whip up something that would make sure nothing in that building will walk out of it?"

"Oh, aye," O'Brian said, snapping his fingers. "I know exactly what'll cure what ails ya this time, laddy," he said with a grunting laugh under his breath. "Give me a few precious moments to confer with the Almighty, and I'll have something for ya straight away, Sergeant."

Sure enough, in less than twenty minutes, O'Brian returned with a small wooden cask tucked up under his right arm, a spool of wire under his left arm, and a toolbox in his left hand. Setting the toolbox down beside one of the other undamaged storefronts, he shoved a stick through the center of the spool, and continued in our direction to the village tavern.

"Hold this, lad," he said, handing me the spool of wire. "Unroll another twenty or so feet of that if you'd be so kind, Sergeant."

I unrolled the wire, while he pulled the cork from the bunghole at the top of the cask, and shoved a heavy gauge wire through the cork in two places.

"Can you cut off the wire and hand it here please?"

I did as he asked. We all watched with morbid fascination as O'Brian split the wires and stripped the insulation from the cut end. He looked up in surprise at all of us. "Sure as I'm still breathing, each and every one of you should be hiding way back over that away. By the church would most likely be the best bet for a safe distance."

We all looked around at each other with shocked surprise.

"Alright, see, when I plug these two wires into the concoction I have in this cask, it'll be ready go *boom*," he said with a flair of his hand. "So unless you're ready to go up on high and meet the Almighty himself, I'd suggest you retreat to a safe distance, sir," he said directly to the lieutenant.

"That's probably some sound advice we'd be smart to follow," Rustay said as he started to walk away. "Everyone back to the trucks!"

"Except the sergeant," O'Brian said.

"Except me?"

"Alright, keep the sergeant if you need to," Rustay said, continuing at a slow jog in the direction of the church.

"Aye, Sergeant. I need you to be ready to latch this door closed while I run my ass over to that box back there," he said, nodding in the direction of the toolbox he'd placed by the building down the street.

"That doesn't sound like the smartest of ideas to me," I said.

"It is." He nodded, then smiled wide. "Trust me."

"Now I *really* don't like this idea."

"See now, what you'll do is open this door when I'm ready," he said, feathering the strands of wires out on the underside of the cork, then placing it back into the bunghole of the cask. "I'll run in, set this wee present down in the middle of those nasty beasties, and then I plan to run like the devil himself is trying to crawl up me arse. Once I clear the door, you shut and bar it with that there latch, then follow behind me and try to keep up." His eyes widened with an excited smile as he chuckled. "Once you're behind the wall with me, I'll set the wee gift basket off, and *Boom!* Bob's your uncle." He picked up the cask and held it at the ready.

"Wait, how do you know that'll work?"

He laughed. "Are you kidding, lad? I don't. I'm just making this shite up as we go. Now open the bloody door and get the fuck out of my way; this thing isn't exactly light."

I pulled back the door and waited at the ready as the stocky Irishman quickly waddled into the tavern, set down the cask, and shot out of the doorway as fast as his legs would carry him. He held his bowler hat down on his head as he sprinted across the distance.

I closed the door, latched it, and followed O'Brian as if I were in hot pursuit. He flung open the top of the box, quickly wrapped the end of the unconnected wire to a post, then flipped up the safety latch on the detonator plunger.

"Ready?" The wild-eyed Irishman pulled upward on the handle, then quickly slammed it back down. The whining whir of the magneto inside the detonator box was quickly overshadowed by the cacophony of Hell on Earth O'Brian had created.

The concussion of the explosion pounded deep down inside my head. I shook my head, then looked around the side of our hiding place. A small crater and a low, ankle-high wall of stone that marked where the tavern had once stood was all that remained. The men by the church whooped and cheered, and then scrambled for cover as bits of stone, wood, and meaty creature chucks indiscriminately fell from on high all around the village.

"See, lad," O'Brian said proudly. He smacked me across the chest with the back of his hand. "I told you it would work." He laughed, then made his way over to the crater to admire his handiwork. He breathed deeply of the smoldering ruins. "Take it in, lad. Breathe it all in. There's nothing like the smell of devastation to fill the soul and stir the blood."

"It's starting to get a bit late," the lieutenant said as he stopped beside me. "What would you think if we finished clearing out this village and hunkered down in the church for the night?"

Shading my eyes, I looked up at the nearly setting sun, then nodded back to the LT. "That would probably be the best idea. We just have to keep our fingers crossed that no Germans come snooping around looking for what caused that explosion."

"I think we'll be alright for the night." He slapped me on the shoulder, then continued on to inspect the building-sized crater we'd created at the end of the village.

In no time we had the carnage cleared from the church, and got ourselves comfortable for the evening just as the sun set below the horizon. Perunko had started a fire in a small cast iron stove at the back of the building and found a pot and some coffee in one of the nearby shops. We'd gone through all the houses in the village, but didn't find any survivors. It looked as if most everyone had been in the village square when the creatures attacked.

What we did find during our search efforts were luxuries to those living in a war zone. Sticks of cured hard sausages, cheeses coated in wax, and even freshly baked cookies that were still set out on a cooling rack in the kitchen of one of the small cottages. That night we ate like kings. After eating our fill, we all stretched out and relaxed. During my search efforts, I'd come across one fine luxury I was sure everyone would enjoy. The bottle of aged scotch was happily received as I took a long sip, then passed it to O'Brian.

"What we have here, ladies and gentlemen, you may never again see in your lifetimes, unless you are lucky enough to survive this war," I said as I produced a small wooden box from my pack. "What I have, contained within the confines of this small but priceless box, may just bring you back to some form of normality."

I held out the box and turned it over so all could see, then slowly opened the top. I eagerly retrieved a long, sweet-smelling cigar from within and passed the delicate brown treat under my nose. Closing the box, I passed it off to O'Brian, then licked the end of the cigar and lit it.

Thick white smoke rolled from my mouth as I puffed. "Take one if you want it and pass the box back around," I said with an odd slur around the cigar that stuck out the side of my mouth.

"So what are you going to do when you get back to the States?" one of the drivers said, asking no one in particular.

I cringed at those words and suddenly found myself back in that barn, listening to Russo complain while they played spades. I shook my head to clear the memories of that night from my mind.

"Hey, Sarge," Doyle said. "What about you? Any big plans when the war is over and you're back in the good ole U S of A?"

"I dunno," I said with a roll of my eyes as I thought about the question. "You never know, I might just decide to stay in the Army."

"Ah, so a lifer with career goals," Pierce said, and laughed.

"It actually sounds kinda boring when you say it like that," Perunko added.

"What the hell," the other driver said and quickly stood from where he had been reclined back on his pack in one of the pews. He stared awkwardly upward.

"What the hell what?" Pierce stood and joined him, looking upward.

"I could have sworn I just saw something up there move."

"That's the whiskey talking," O'Brian said, then took another sip from the bottle before passing it on.

"You're probably just tired, Private." Rustay walked over and placed a hand on the young man's shoulder.

"We've had a few long and stressful days. Why don't you go ahead and turn in for the night?"

"Maybe you're right, LT. I think I will," the private said. "It was just strange. I could have sworn I saw that gargoyle thing move its head up there." He laid back down and got comfortable against his pack.

"Gargoyle? I don't remember seeing any gargoyles in here." I looked upward in the direction the private had been staring and saw another of the creatures gazing down at us. It turned its head in my direction, and I could have sworn it smiled. It dove from its perch to the private and tore open the man's chest with no effort. The soldier was dead before he realized what had happened to him.

"They're in the church!" I instinctually drew my revolver, cocked the hammer, and fired a large caliber round into the thing.

Widowmakers

Chapter 7

Digging a grave is never an easy thing to do, let alone for someone under your command. Even though we barely knew the guy, the gruesome death of Corporal Bowman, a kid in his early twenties from Arkansas, struck a dark chord in each of our souls. It gave us a glimpse into our own deeply repressed fears and our sense of mortality. It's never an easy thing to stare the Reaper in the face while he grins back at you, even if it's just in the back of your mind.

We policed the area and triple checked every nook and cranny of the village for more of the creatures before we set to work with the digging. Each one of us, including the lieutenant, took their turn removing one shovel full after another of the rich black earth, which would soon embrace our brother in arms for the rest of eternity. Once we'd dug down to about waist deep, we went about preparing Bowman for burial.

Doyle found a beautifully stitched quilt in one of the quaint cottages on the outskirts of the village that we used to wrap the corporal in. Lieutenant Rustay removed the corporal's tags and said a few kind words by the graveside, while O'Brian quietly sang "Amazing Grace" in his comforting Irish lilt. Most everyone joined in, singing quietly or under their breath. Even though none of us really knew the guy, more than a few of us wept, myself included. I don't know if it was the sweet sound of the song on the air, the fear of the unknown that hid in the eerily dark night, or the fact that we were all, in fact, mortal.

We carefully placed Corporal Bowman in the shallow pit, backfilled the hole, and covered the grave in fieldstones, creating a small cairn to mark his resting place. No one really slept that night. We napped and rested our eyes, but that was about the extent of it. Whether from fear, anxious anticipation, or that ever-present thought of death that lingered over a man in a war zone, none of us could sleep.

Since there were bound to be more of the creatures out there, Lieutenant Rustay decided to continue searching for any signs by following a long loop around the area that would eventually take us back to Omaha Beach. Just before daybreak, the LT and Pierce spoke in low tones as they planned the return route back to base. They examined a map the LT had laid out over the altar at the far end of the sanctuary.

At one point, Rustay looked up from the map and caught me watching him and Pierce. He glanced around the room to see who else was awake, then motioned for me.

"O'Brian, Sullivan. I need you both over here, please."

I obliged the LT, nudging O'Brian with the toe of my boot as I walked past him. He woke with a start and looked up at me with confusion-filled eyes. I gave him a sideways nod in the direction of the LT, then continued over to the altar. O'Brian followed right behind me. Groggily rubbing his eyes, he howled as he let out a long, stretched yawn.

"Morning, fellas," Rustay said, looking up from the map. "I hope both of you managed to get some rest."

"As much as I could," I said, glancing down at the map.

"Oh, aye, Sir. Just a wee nap here and there is all."

"Good, because I need you two to scout ahead for us and see what we might be driving into. It looks like the direction the creatures were heading will take them on a direct path to the village of Mouen. I want to go there next and see what we can find out from the locals."

"If there are any left," Pierce added.

"We'll follow this road north, around these fields," Rustay said, pointing at the map. "I want the two of you to continue following the path of the creatures across these fields and forested areas. But whatever you do, do *not* put yourselves into any unnecessary danger."

"Not a problem, LT," I said, looking up from the map. "When do you want us to be on the move?"

"Preferably as soon as the sun is up. I'd rather you get a good head start on the trucks, so if you run into anything ahead, you'll have time to come back and warn us."

"Sure enough, sir, it'll be easy enough for the two of us."

"Good," Rustay said. "Move out as soon as you're ready."

We both quickly ate from the previous night's feast and drank enough of the now thick but still warm coffee from the night before to wake ourselves fully. Before the sun had broken the horizon, we set out on our course northwest along the Avenue des Capelles. We walked along the road for about a half a mile, then left the pavement cutting across a potato field, making a beeline for a stand of trees in the distance. By this time the sun had broken the horizon, and the clouds were afire with the burning reds and purples of morning. The path of the creatures was obvious. Besides the destruction that had been wrought on the field crops, the strange, three-toed footprints dotted the loose soil of the field.

You'd be surprised at the similarities between the countryside of Walker County, Georgia, and Northern France. Fields as far as the eye can see. Low hills that hid at the edge of the misty distance. Even down to the smell of wheat, rye, and hay straw mixed with the fresh scent of wildflowers on the wind. It's honestly just enough to make me homesick, like I could take a turn down the next bend, go down a rutted dirt road, and be at my Granny's house. Hell, I can smell the soup beans and cornbread she's had cooking all afternoon for dinner. And the fresh-baked strawberry rhubarb pie sitting there in the windowsill, teasing every one of us with its tangy-sweet scent as it cooled. You sure as hell didn't dare to stick your finger in it. If Granny caught you messing with any of her fresh pies, she'd light your ass up real quick with that old wooden spoon she uses for everything, including an ass-whoopin'.

"Sure enough, if we aren't careful, this entire situation could go arseways on us in a heartbeat," O'Brian said as he slid back the bolt on his Enfield rifle, checked the round, and closed the breech.

"You ain't kidding," I said as I swung my M1 Garand around on its sling and off my shoulder. I checked my weapon, then slung it back over my shoulder. "So what's your story, O'Brian? You really haven't said much about your life before the war."

"There really isn't much to tell," he said without breaking stride across the field. "I grew up working on a farm, tending to pigs and crops. Wasn't much, but we worked hard, and we were there for one another." He hitched up his rucksack and tightened the shoulder straps. "We should pick up the pace if we're going to beat the layabouts riding in the trucks." He rocked his head side to side until his neck let out a loud crack, then broke into a brisk trot. I sprinted to catch up and easily kept pace with the short Irishman. He held his rifle in one hand, and with his other, held the battered and dirty bowler hat on top off his head. It was a sight to see. Like watching a leprechaun sprint for the end of the rainbow, protecting his pot of gold. With the exception of low fieldstone walls in our path, we easily jogged through the nearly ready to harvest fields of wheat, and had crossed a mile or so, before coming upon a farmhouse in our path, south of the village of Mouen.

We slowed to a steady walk and ducked behind a field wall to catch our breath. We both eagerly took out our canteens. I panted and gasped between sips of water, while O'Brian barely looked winded.

"Don't worry none, lad. Mark my words, I'll toughen you up before the war is over." He laughed and took a long drink from his canteen.

"Suppose it would be a good idea to give farmhouses a wide berth," I said, then dryly swallowed. "I wouldn't want to scare the locals any more than they already are, or give them a reason to shoot at us.

Abruptly, a discordant howl of terror sailed over the landscape from the small farmhouse. We looked to one another in utter surprise, then back in the direction of the woman's scream.

"We've a mission, Lad," O'Brian said, shaking his head as his gaze searched the outside of the small farmhouse.

"We also have a duty," I said with a stern glare at the Irishman.

His shoulders slumped with a heavy sigh, then he looked up at me. "There'll be no talking you out of it either, I suppose?"

"Nope," I said and quickly clambered over the low stone wall. Crouching, I sprinted across the distance to the nearest corner of the small stone farmhouse. As I crept closer to the window on the field side of the building, I could hear the sound of boots scuffling on a wooden floor, and strangled, gasping breaths.

A woman incoherently sobbed and shouted something in French, then began wailing from inside the cottage.

"Let go of her, you damned bloody barbarians!" Even while shouting, the man's voice carried an aristocratic tone of British finality. "I'm speaking to the two of you bloody damned Jerrys! I said let her go!"

"Können wir den pompösen Esel dieses Tommy schon noch töten? Sein Gejammer bereitet mir Kopfschmerzen," a man said in German.

"Absolut nicht! Er ist ein Offizier. Es gibt wahrscheinlich eine Belohnung dafür, ihn lebend hereinzubringen," another male voice said from inside the cottage.

Beyond the screams of the woman as she fought against one of the Germans inside the cottage was a muffled thud accompanied by a painful sounding *umph*. Very slowly and very quietly, we crept our way up to the window and slowly stood, peeking in just as a German soldier lifted a British captain off the floor by his collar and punched him in the side of the head with the butt of his pistol, then shoved him back to the floor. The other soldier held the woman down on the ancient-looking wooden table, strangling her with both of his gloved hands. She kicked and slapped at his hands, unable to break the soldier's grip, as she fought for the slightest breath of fresh air. With what looked like little effort, the soldier lifted her from the table and threw her against the front door. The walls of the stone cottage shook from the impact as she slammed into the door.

The soldier strutted as he walked around the table and placed his hat on a nearby shelf, then began unbuttoning his uniform top. She shouted something in French that I didn't understand in his general direction, spit, then darted out the door.

We ducked out of sight below the window, and I looked over to see that O'Brian had already drawn his trench knife and was inching forward toward the corner of the cottage. One of the German soldiers laughed, followed by loud chatter between the pair of them.

The sound of a sliding footstep in gravel drew our attention back to the side of the house, where the French woman stared blankly down at us. Her mouth worked wordlessly like a fish out of water. All three of us heard the door of the cottage creak open, to the raucous laugh of one of the Germans. Quickly I grabbed the woman by the arm and pulled her to the ground, covering her mouth. O'Brian moved around me toward the corner of the building, gently placing his hat on the woman's head as he did. His knife at the ready, he crouched like a coiled copperhead ready to strike at an unsuspecting victim in that asshole way they tend to do.

I could hear one of the soldiers softly cooing something in German as he came around the side of the structure.

"Bloody fucking Jerrys!" the British soldier shouted. I could hear him struggling with the other German, when a solid sounding thump was followed by the sound of something heavy falling to the wooden floor.

O'Brian leapt upward, sinking the blade of his trench knife up to the brass knuckle hilt into the unsuspecting soldier's throat. The woman's muscles tightened at the sudden sight of gushing blood that flowed down O'Brian's arms. I felt her stomach contracted with an involuntary heave from the coppery scent of blood that abruptly found its way to us. The soldier's mouth wordlessly moved, grasping for any sound. He gurgled and gasped, then limply collapsed forward onto the short Irishman. O'Brian lowered the soldier to the ground and dragged him back toward where I hunkered down with the French lady. After pulling the German's feet around the corner, O'Brian turned in our direction, and stared, almost mesmerized at the dark red blood that stained and began to congeal on his hands. He flexed his fingers, making fists, then stretching them out again. The look of contentment on his face made me think he was savoring the feel it as it hardened on his skin. He drunkenly leaned his head in our direction, then smiled and let out a long, satisfied sigh.

"Merry meet, and merry part, and merry meet again," O'Brian whispered then took a deep breath. "He is with the fae and within their realm now. It is they who will reckon and adjudicate his soul. Sláinte," he said with a nod.

The French woman struggled in my grasp. I held my hand over her mouth, muffling the panic-filled scream I was sure she would let out.

O'Brian knelt next to me and the woman. He silently placed a blood-covered finger to his lips, motioning for her to be quiet. Cold, calculating calmness stemmed from his dark, beady eyes. A calm serenity washed over me at the sound of O'Brian's voice as he spoke to the woman in soft tones of French beautifully sheathed with an Irish lilt.

I felt her entire body clench, then suddenly relax, as if his words were a comforting release. She nodded slightly.

"My French is a little rusty," I said, my eyes unmoving from the Irishman.

"She understands and can speak English," he whispered without breaking eye contact. "You're safe, lass. We'll take you out of here with us."

"Bloody hell, my head is splitting," the British officer said from inside the cottage. We easily heard the grunted strikes of the other German soldier as he kicked the British officer.

O'Brian closed his eyes and took a deep, calming breath. His gaze suddenly popped up, staring straight at me. "Keep her quiet while I finish this." He turned, withdrew his knife from the corpse of the other soldier, and disappeared around the corner of the building.

I released the woman and removed my hand from her mouth. She started to sit up, then tensed at the sudden sound of another wet gurgle, followed by a heavy thud from inside the cottage.

Moments later O'Brian reappeared at the corner of the cottage, swiping blood away with two fingers from the blade of his trench knife. "We're clear, lad."

The woman started to sob. Her entire body shook with crying laughter. She wrapped her arms around my neck and crawled up into my lap. She was a half-starved, frail looking thing. I could feel every rib along her back when I wrapped my arms around her in a comforting embrace. I gently rocked her back and forth as she cried into my chest.

"Bloody hell," O'Brian said. "Leave it to the American to do nothing and still get the lass."

"Oh, ha ha," I said. "What was I supposed to do? I'm open to suggestions if you've got any."

O'Brian laughed, then put away his knife. He knelt and searched through the soldier's pockets. "I'd have done the same, lad."

I stood, easily lifting the small woman who hung from my neck, and carried her into the house. Just inside the door, the body of the other German lay bleeding out on the bare wooden planks.

"Let me get that out of your way," O'Brian said as he grabbed the soldier by the feet and dragged him outside.

I turned one of the chairs upright with my foot, then carefully set the woman down on it, detaching her from my neck. I glanced about for a water pitcher or hand pump. It was a quaint two-room cottage house that reminded me of my Granny's place. Small, compact, but full of life and stories of the family. Small trinkets decorated spaces between the utilitarian tools of a working farm kitchen. I unscrewed my canteen and handed it to her. She took the offering with a grunted nod and sipped. I crouched next to her and looked her over for injuries.

"What can we do to help you? Is there someone we can take you to?"

She stared blankly at me.

"Her wits are addled," O'Brian said as he returned to the cottage. "You may not be able to get through to her."

I turned and looked back at the Irishman, then nodded in the direction of the British officer. "See if he's still breathing. Maybe he can tell us something." I lifted the canteen back to her lips and spoke softly, "Take another sip. When you're ready to talk, we'd like to know about those soldiers."

She took the canteen back and sipped, her eyes darting back and forth between me and O'Brian.

"We aren't going to hurt you. We're the good guys," I said and flashed her what I thought was my best lady-killer smile.

She laughed, choking slightly on the water. "Does that look work for you in the States? Because you look like a sad little puppy," she said with a heavy French accent.

"I don't think anything works for him, lass. He's too damned homely for any of that."

"Oh, thanks a lot, O'Brian." I shot him a perturbed glance.

"O'Brian," she said with a nod toward the Irishman then turned to me with a questioning look.

"My name is Grady Sullivan," I said. "Pleased to meet you, Ma'am." I extended my hand to shake.

"April Chevrolet," she said, taking my offered hand.

I must have looked at her strangely or something, because she immediately offered an excuse.

"Yes, the same as the American car company," she said. "He may be a distant relation, but I honestly have no idea."

"Huh," I grunted. "You learn something new every day. I had no idea the founder of Chevrolet Motors was French.

"Most of you Americans are ignorant of anything that isn't American." She let out a disdainful sigh. Her eyes narrowed as she glared in my direction.

Widowmakers

I quickly gathered my thoughts and changed the subject before she could become confrontational. I looked down at my watch, then out the window at the sun as it rose ever higher in the sky. "We really need to get moving. What about the soldiers?"

She looked suspiciously between the two of us, her jaw muscles clenched as she chewed on her thoughts, then let out a reluctant breath. "The soldiers arrived here just a short time before the two of you. I have no idea what direction they came from." She looked down at the British captain sprawled out on the floor. "They may have been chasing him," she said, glaring down the bridge of her nose at the motionless form.

I turned and looked at the officer, then back to April. "Where did he come from?"

"We ran into each other along the road last night. I was on my way to my grandmother's in Mouen when he appeared out of nowhere, sprinting across the road. He slid to a stop, then took my hand and dragged me along with him. He kept babbling about goblins and imps that were chasing him. At first I thought him to be a mad man. How could I believe him? I tried to pull myself free from his grip, but he was too strong for me. I had no choice but to run and try to keep up with him. If I had fallen, I think he might have continued to drag me along the ground."

A shiver washed over her small frame, then she sucked in a breath and pulled herself free from the thought. She took another sip of water and continued.

"If I hadn't seen them with my own eyes, I would have thought him mad, but they were real. Small and brown, with rows of teeth. The one that leapt onto my back had three fingers on its clawed hand, and some of them had these bat-like wings. We escaped and managed to find this cottage. We forced our way in and barred the door. The Nazis arrived only this morning and took us by surprise."

"Well, we're on our way to Mouen to meet with our convoy. You're welcome to join us."

"Lucky for you we happened along when we did," O'Brian said. He leaned over the British officer, examining him. "I think he might be waking up, Sergeant."

The officer blindly swung as his eyes opened wide with surprise. "Bloody fucking hell!" He scrambled back, then looked over at April and me. "So that's the bloody secret to why you Americans do what you do so well. You've summoned the likes of devils and leprechauns to do your dirty work." He looked back to O'Brian, focusing on the British uniform the Irishman wore, and angrily glared at him. "It is a sad day for the Empire when our ranks have been soiled by the likes of a potato eater."

"Oh, aye." O'Brian smiled wide. "You think so, do you, *Captain*? How's about I just pop back out and find a few Jerrys to replace the two who were beating your sorry arse."

"Enough!" I stood and pulled my rucksack back over my shoulders. "We're all in the shit together. Let's get moving so we can meet up with the convoy."

"I'll not be talked to like that by any enlisted man, let alone a bloody fucking Yank. Who exactly do you think you are?"

"*Staff Sergeant* Grady Sullivan of the United States Army Air Corps, *sir*," I said with a snap of a salute. "And I'll tell you what, Captain. I couldn't give two shits if you stay or go, that's your call. But we're heading to Mouen." I turned back to April. "Are you coming with us?"

She stood, smoothing her dress, then crossed her arms. "I will gladly take my leave of this place."

I started out the door and cocked my head toward O'Brian. "Let's put some distance between us and here."

"Aye, Sergeant. I'd be bloody fucking happy to."

I set the pace at a steady fast walk. O'Brian fell in line behind me, while April hiked up her skirts and jogged forward to walk beside me.

"I know you aren't used to trudging through fields at an Army pace, but unless you say something, I'll press on at a decent speed. We need to put some miles behind us if we're going to scout things out before the trucks come through."

"I'll be perfectly fine, Sergeant." She flashed a challenging smile at me.

"I don't suppose you blokes would mind if I tagged along, would you?" The British officer jogged up alongside April, then slowed, catching his breath.

I heard O'Brian scoff at the Brit.

I picked up the pace to a fast jog through the waist-high field of grains. "Keep up, keep your mouth shut, and you'll do just fine, *sir*."

Chapter 8

We'd crossed the next two miles of fields in what I thought was record time. April, the young French woman, had kept up with O'Brian and me with little trouble. The British officer, Captain Reginald Sizemore the *Third*, who had profusely expressed the importance of being the *Third*, had joined our ranks and barely managed to keep up, collapsing by the time we took a rest break just outside the village of Mouen. During the trek, O'Brian had a slight slip of the tongue, calling the captain a turd instead of the third. By the dark shades of red his face had turned, I could have sworn the top of the captain's head was going to explode. The man must have had a condition that caused him to run off at the mouth when he was nervous or stressed, because even though he was gasping for air during our two-mile run, he insisted that we needed to know about him and his family.

Captain Sizemore was the eldest son of Reginald Sizemore the Second, of the Nottingham Sizemores. He insisted that they weren't really rich, but they were comfortably well off. His father had made a decent name for himself and amassed a small fortune, investing in the shipbuilding industry. He had lucked into a deal back in the spring of 1912 and bought hundreds of shares in the White Star Line for pennies on the dollar just after the sinking of the Titanic. He continued to regale us with this or that moment of notoriety or briefest of meetings with members of the royal family.

After a short rest to let the good captain catch his breath, we continued for what had to be another half mile through an ancient hardwood forest. Thick oaks and elms covered the landscape. Their canopies were so thick they nearly blocked out the sun, stunting the development of all but the most tenacious of undergrowth. We left the tree line behind, crossing one last field of wheat as we approached the village, only to climb a rise and find the burnt ruins of the village of Mouen.

The stone walls of the structures remained as markers to what must have been a picturesque postcard setting. Luckily we didn't find the remains of anyone in the village, but there were two German half-tracks parked in the center of the village that looked like they'd lost a fight with a grizzly bear. Parts and pieces of the armored vehicles were scattered about the area. Just like the villagers, there was no sign of the Germans. We completed our search through what remained of the village, then found a spot on the eastern side to settle down and rest while we waited for the convoy to arrive. I fetched a bucket of water from the village well, while O'Brian started a small fire, so we could heat up a few rations for April and Captain Sizemore.

While we waited, April broke the awkward silence by mentioning that if her grandmother and sister weren't here, they'd most likely have continued to Christot, to the northwest. She had an uncle who lived there, whom her grandmother would have gone to visit if things had gotten bad. I didn't have a good feeling about that. When we'd searched the village, we found the path of destruction wrought by the creatures had taken them toward the northwest. O'Brian looked up at me about the same time I looked at him when she mentioned the direction. A knot settled in the pit of my stomach, and I changed the subject by asking Captain Sizemore why he was out in the French countryside, wandering about on his own.

He eagerly jumped at the opportunity to enlighten and regale us with the story of being appointed to the L Detachment of the British Special Air Service. He said his superiors had loved each of the ideas he'd submitted to higher headquarters, and they were thoroughly impressed with the tenacious resolve he'd shown when faced with each of the dozens of rejections. Sizemore dug around in an inner pocket of his field jacket and produced the acceptance letter he'd received from headquarters just prior to this mission. He proudly passed it around and showed each of us, pointing out the signature of Major David Stirling at the bottom of the page. His detailed plans of misdirection and misinformation, which had to be executed in theater, led to his almost immediate deployment aboard one of the many C-47 Skytrains that rained down personnel behind enemy lines across the French countryside. He was to implement his elaborate plans and wreak havoc on the enemy from behind the lines. While listening to this, I wasn't sure if they actually had faith in the guy, or if they wanted to quietly dispose of him for being an annoying asshole.

Less than an hour later, we could hear the roar of the trucks' diesel engines in the distance. They lumbered slowly down the unpaved roads, carefully navigating the holes and ruts across the road's uneven surface. They pulled in and parked the trucks in the middle of the road beside where we'd set up our small cook fire.

"Sullivan!" Lieutenant Rustay unfolded his map as he slid from the passenger seat of the transport truck. "What have you found? And who are they?" He tipped his head with a sidelong glance in the direction of April and Captain Sizemore when he noticed the British officer approaching.

I motioned for April and the others to remain where they were as I headed in the direction of the Lieutenant. "Survivors we found just south of here. They escaped from the creatures only to be attacked by a pair of German soldiers. The girl is searching for her grandmother and her little sister; the captain…" I shrugged as Sizemore stopped before the two of us and snapped himself to attention.

Rustay popped to attention, saluted, and tucked the map under his arm. "I'm Lieutenant Rustay of Task Force 13," he said, extending his hand.

"Captain Reginald Sizemore the Third, at your service," he said with a clack of his heels, returning the salute. "I'll gladly offer my service wherever I can help, Lieutenant."

"That's appreciated, Captain. If you'll go ahead and load up, we'll be moving on shortly."

The captain grumbled and harrumphed under his breath. "If I may ask, Lieutenant, in what direction are we heading?"

"Back to Chippelle Airfield, near Omaha Beach."

"Ah, excellent, Lieutenant. Excellent," Sizemore said and started to head for the truck, then stopped and turned back. "Please let me know if I may be of help in any way, Lieutenant," he said with a slight bow, then climbed into the truck.

Rustay turned to me with a look of confused consternation.

"Tell me about it," I said. "At least he didn't try to talk your ear off."

"So what did you and O'Brian find out?"

"Not too much, really. Just that the creatures have been through here. They aren't trying to hide their tracks in the least. We haven't found any survivors here, so they either escaped, or were taken by the things.

Widowmakers

"Any remains?" Rustay glanced up from his map with a look of concern.

"Not this time, so I'm guessing most everyone got out. Er...well, I'm at least hoping they did. The trail of the creatures heads off toward the northwest."

Rustay went back to examining his map; he unfolded it and held it up against the side of the truck so I could easily see. "I don't know what's driving them along. Maybe they're migrating or something? But you'd think that world would know about it if this was a regular occurrence."

"I'm leaning toward hornet's nest, sir."

"What do you mean?" Rustay looked back at me again.

"You ever tossed rocks at a hornet's nest before?"

"What? No. Why would anyone in their right mind piss off a nest of hornets?"

"That's exactly my point," I said. "What if these things are normally hidden away and only come out on occasion? So far it looks like they nest in caves or in the ground. What if all the noise of the war has stirred them up like throwing rocks at a hornet's nest?"

"You do make a good point, Sullivan. But we need to get back," Rustay said, turning back to the map again. "If we head north along the Rue de Caligny, assuming the roads are clear, we could be back to the airfield sometime tomorrow."

"What about the creatures? We can't just let the trail go cold."

"We also need to establish our base of operations, unless we want to be assimilated back into the Regular Army." Rustay traced a route across the map with his finger.

"What about the girl? We can't just leave her here by herself."

"She can go back to the base with us and be relocated from there as she wishes. But for now, she'll be safe."

"Let me take one of the trucks and run her back over to her uncle's farm at least. She said it is over near Christot, so it wouldn't be too far out of the way."

"We can't rescue every damsel in distress, Sullivan."

"I know that, LT. But it's on our way back, not horribly out of the way, and it's still in the direction of those things. Maybe if I'm lucky, I can find their new nest site, and we can blow the shit out of it. What would it hurt? We might could save some other folks from a fate worse than the Nazis and learn more about these critters."

Rustay quietly thought for a moment, then agreed. "You drop her if her people are there. If they aren't, go ahead and bring her back to base, and she can find her way from there."

"You've got a deal, LT!"

"Take the rear truck, it has the least amount of salvage on board, and we can move some of the smaller stuff to the other trucks, too. If you're captured or killed, it's less of a loss for the rest of us," Rustay said with a wink and a slap to my shoulder.

"Thanks, LT. You won't regret this." I slapped him across the shoulder and hurried back over to where April and O'Brian were still seated along the roadside.

"Might be a good idea to hose Pierce down before he hurts himself," O'Brian said jokingly as I walked up.

April sat on the fallen log with her legs crossed and her hands wrapped comfortably around her knee as she listened intently to Pierce's tale. "Warrant Officer Pierce was just explaining to me how he was shot down while on a reconnaissance mission, searching for Nazi convoys," April said teasingly. "But I was just thinking that if he were shot down, he must not be a very good pilot in the first place. Would this be true?"

O'Brian let out a hearty chuckle.

"Hey, Sullivan," Pierce said as I approached, holding out his hand in greeting.

I took his hand and shook. "Guess the LT hasn't gotten tired of you yet."

"Lucky for me he hasn't," he said, laughing.

"It's your lucky day," I said with a smile as I turned to April. "The LT has given me permission to take one of the trucks and carry you to your uncle's farm." I looked to O'Brian and nodded. "Are you up for a side trip to take her back and to follow the trail of those things?"

"Oh, aye. It'd be better than going back to base and unloading these trucks."

"Pierce? What about you? Wanna tag along?" I slapped the Navy pilot across the arm, bringing him out of his daze as he stared at April.

"What?" He stood, startled, and turned to me. "What was that? I didn't quite catch it."

"The LT gave me permission to take one of the trucks and carry April to her uncle's farm. You wanna tag along, or would you rather go back to base?" The look of thought that crossed his face told me his answer before he even opened his mouth. The man was horribly smitten with the young French girl and would probably do anything she asked him to do.

After a short break, the LT was ready to get back on the road. We climbed into the truck and parted ways with the rest of the team just outside the village. We continued west, while they turned to the north. I'm sure we were making better time than the others, since our truck had very little extra weight in it, and the roadway wasn't horribly rutted out. We crossed the winding ten-mile distance of the French countryside in under two hours. Instead of rushing to drop April at her uncle's farm, we took our time to look around for any signs of the creatures. The crisscrossing path of the creatures that we'd passed over more than a few times led right into the small village of Cristot.

We pulled up to the charred remains of the village in the early afternoon. It was almost identical to the scenes we'd come across before. Burnt beams smoldered among the ruins of stone-walled buildings. Scattered remains of both livestock and villagers looked like they'd been gnawed on and were scattered all about the village.

O'Brian let out a long whistle. "Would you bloody look at that! I'd sure as tomorrow say those little beasties have been through here."

April muttered something in French while crossing herself as the realization of what she was looking at struck her.

"This is a hell of a lot more destruction than we've seen anywhere else," I said. "Is it just me, or is it starting to look like there are more of them?"

Pierce climbed down from the truck and kicked at some of the still-smoldering debris laying on top of a partially-eaten torso. "Why are there so many parts left this time?" He turned back to look at us in the truck. "They didn't carry any of the meat with them back to their den like the last time."

"Yeah, you're right." I slid from the seat of the truck to the ground. "They left bits and pieces before, but nothing like this. I mean, there's half a cow laying over there against that fence," I said with a nod in that direction as I knelt beside Pierce. I examined the rotund, shirtless torso and shoulder. "He sure as hell looks chewed on. Almost like a pack of coyotes got hold of the poor bastard."

"Grand-mère Monette," April gasped and leapt from the cab of the truck. Hiking her skirts, she darted away down a side path that led around to the far side of the village.

"April, wait!" Pierce shouted, chasing behind her. He grabbed her by the arm and spun her around to face him.

"If anyone survived, they would have taken shelter in the tower." She tore her arm from his grip and continued, storming away in the direction of the squat tower/keep structure that peeked above the scorched walls of the village.

"Sergeant?" O'Brian shouted in a questioning tone.

I turned back to see him gathering dead chickens from the ground.

"What about all this meat?" The Irishman lifted one of the mangled birds to his nose and sniffed at the stiff carcass. "They're still fresh enough to eat." He shrugged.

"Kick up a fire and knock yourself out, O'Brian. We need to take care of these bodies before we leave, too. Pierce, give him a hand while I check out this tower." I turned and continued down the side path between buildings in pursuit of the young French woman. As I rounded the building and followed the path, a squat spire that tapered into the heavens came into full view. Constructed mostly of what looked like cut field stones, the structure rose only a few stories into the sky and loomed above the green field surrounding it. April pulled with all her might at an iron ring embedded in the ancient wooden door. She grunted and tugged without result.

"I'd say that's probably a promising sign."

Widowmakers

She stopped, dropping the door ring with a frustrated huff, and turned to look back at me. She blew puffs of air upward, then swiped an annoying wisp of hair from her face. She crossed her arms and glared at me, taking on an angry but defensive stance. "And how exactly could the door being jammed be a good sign?"

"Because it isn't jammed," I said and stepped over to the door. Using the butt of my field knife, I rapped on the heavy oak door. I could hear the distinctive sound of steel sliding against wood on the other side.

"Américain stupide. What good will knocking do if they are trapped inside?"

The sound of latches sliding away resounded from the door and I turned back to her. "It'll do fine if they just locked themselves in." I smiled at her, then turned back to the door as it opened just a crack. A dark-gray eye peered out, scrutinizing me.

The door suddenly flung open as an aged farmer rushed out from the tower entrance, frantically babbling something in French. He embraced me in a desperately thankful hug and lifted me off the ground like I weighed nothing. His babbling continued, almost to the point of sounding like a stutter, as he repeated the same thing over and over in French. April pulled the man away from me, desperately asking him something. I recognized the names of her grandmother and sister amid the flurry of words I didn't otherwise understand in the slightest.

"Grand-mère," she gasped, relief washing over her face as she quickly crossed herself and ran into the ancient stone keep.

I followed close behind as April ascended the narrow stone stairs to the second level. Burlap sacks stacked two deep lined the far wall from the stairwell. Bundles of herbs, open crates of potatoes, and neatly arranged stacks of casks made up the rest of the room's contents. April rushed to the side of an older woman, who was laying across the stacks of grain sacks and looked to have been napping. A young girl I assumed was April's little sister, Carmen, let out a shrill scream and leapt into April's arms.

The older woman woke with a start. "Merci la sainte mère!"

I stepped slowly toward them as April comforted the old woman and, I guessed, explained what was going on. I heard her say my name and glance toward me at one point. The old woman gave me that knowing evil-eyed glance that grandmothers of pretty granddaughters flash about on occasion, especially when the guy on the receiving end of that glare was an American soldier in uniform.

Stepping forward, I looked them over the best I could without getting too close. Neither of them looked to be injured, just tired, and plain worn out. I'm sure the encounter with the creatures had taken a toll on them. Without a doubt it had taken its toll on me.

The old farmer climbed the stairs and said something in French. I looked back to April for an explanation.

"He asked if it is safe for him to leave the keep..." she said with an uncomfortable hum. "He needs to…" Her eyes darted about as she searched her memory for the correct word in English. "He needs to visit the necessary, if it is alright with you."

I thought for a moment, wondering what she could be talking about, then noticed the uncomfortable, almost painful look on his face while he rocked back and forth. Then it hit me like a brick.

"Yes! Oh God, yes! Absolutely! Tell him to take as long as he needs. It'll take us a while to collect the bodies and give them a proper burial."

She said something, and the old farmer immediately turned and sprinted back down the stairs.

"How is your grandmother?"

"Tired, scared, but otherwise healthy." She straightened herself and held her head high in a matronly fashion. "It will take more than a war or creatures to break our spirits," she said proudly.

I smiled and nodded back at her. "If you ladies will excuse me, we've got a bit of work to get done before dark." I nodded and tipped the edge of my helmet toward April's grandmother. "We'll hole up here for the night. Get what you need from the trucks to make her comfortable, and we'll all have a good belly full. Meat, meat, and more meat is on tonight's menu."

Chapter 9

We worked as fast as we physically could until that evening. With the help of the old farmer, we collected the remains of the villagers and buried them in a mass grave near the tower, while April, her little sister Carmen, and Grand-mère Monette cooked the salvageable bits of chicken, mutton, and beef. They had quickly erected a wooden frame over a small fire and cut hundreds of thin slices of meat, which they then hung on the frame over the fire. Larger portions of meat that had been set aside for our dinner slowly cooked over a fire that had been lit in the tower's large fireplace.

When I'd pass by where the ladies were working, I could hear Grand-mère Monette chattering on to April in a cautionary tone. I couldn't understand a lick of what the old lady said, since it was all in French, but for whatever reason, it always seemed like she was giving me the evil eye. Glaring at me whenever I'd look in their direction. I really don't think she liked me, and for the life of me I couldn't figure out why. Maybe because we were Americans invading her homeland, even though we were there to drive back the Nazis from France. Or maybe she half expected me to soil her granddaughter and leave her with child. It wouldn't be the first time something like that happened during a war.

By the time the sun had set, we'd parked the truck just outside the door of the tower, and settled ourselves down for the evening in the first floor of the structure. Using some heavy canvas we'd found upstairs, we covered every murder hole we could to prevent light from escaping and giving us away. The scent of cooking meat hung heavy in the orange glow of the keep.

Pierce had gathered a respectable stack of firewood for the womenfolk before the night settled over us. Each trip back into the tower with an armload of wood was an opportunity for him to say a word or two, or to steal another glance at April. If he was trying to hide his interest in her, he was going about it horribly. If looks could kill, the daggers Grand-mère Monette flashed at him when he'd bring in another load of wood would have done him in on the first trip. He sat near the fireplace, stoking and feeding the fire as needed to maintain the heat to cure the remainder of the meat. He hung on April's every word, even the French ones, as he tried to remember and translate each of them.

After we'd all eaten, those of us with smokes lit up, and O'Brian passed around his canteen, which had miraculously refilled itself once again.

I let out a slight chuckle at a long-forgotten memory. "This reminds me of when I was little, and we'd spend the evenings at my Granny's house during the summer harvest. We'd all be gathered around the fireplace, where she had this or that cooking on the hearth. My paw and grandpaw would both be smoking their hand-carved pipes while sipping on some of last year's hard cider they'd tapped to see if it was ready to sell off. Even this old tower reminds me of the house my grandpaw built with his own hands from the field stones he'd dug up on their land."

"There was an old tavern the landlord owned near our lease," O'Brian said, then took another sip from his canteen. "My Da would take me and my older brother with him on occasion, when he had business to conduct, so I could learn the fine art of negotiation and to build up my tolerance to drink at the same time." O'Brian let out a laugh under his breath. "Negotiations go oh, so much better when you get the other feller a wee bit sloshed." He winked and held up the canteen in salute, then tipped it back once again.

The old woman muttered something under her breath with a sigh to April, who replied with a shocked start.

"What is it?" I sat up, adjusting myself on the uncomfortable wooden crate.

April's eyes widened. "She…" She let out an exasperated sigh. "Grand-mère Monette does not like any of you. She especially does not like the Irishmen. She'd rather trust the Pouque than trust an Irishman. She said they are all merely liars and thieves, and she will be sleeping with one eye open to make sure he does not steal her soul.

"Pouque?" I stepped over to the fireplace and retrieved a glowing ember to light a cigarette. "I don't know that word. What does it mean?"

She turned back to her grandmother and asked her something in French. The old woman let out a spine-chilling cackle, which sent her into a coughing fit that wracked her entire body. April glanced back to me with an unsure look. Grandmaw finally got control of herself and started explaining to April with a frightened tone. April nodded as the old woman continued and started to translate for me.

"The Pouque are an ancient race of earth spirits who have lived hand in hand with man since time immemorial. Once, long ago, the Pouque were numerous, and could be the bringers of good fortune or ill. It was said you could find them living deep in the stone. The war has disturbed them from their slumber. They are awake once again, and they are angry with the noise of men and the machines they helped to create."

The old woman laughed and coughed, then laid herself down on a bed of grain sacks. She rolled over on her side away from us and snuggled into her younger granddaughter, who was already fast asleep.

"But what are they? We know we can kill them; I've proven that myself," I said. "So they're at least flesh and blood."

"I have heard others speak of them over the years," April said. "I have heard them called imps, goblins, devils, and fae. But what they actually are, I do not know."

"Well, I suppose you can go ahead and add the name 'gremlin' to your list. That's what the Brits called them whenever something suddenly broke on one of their planes."

"That's pretty much what I've heard, too," Pierce added.

"It doesn't seem like they have returned to any of the areas they have already been through."

"Maybe they're migrating, like ducks or geese," O'Brian added.

I shrugged. "At this point, I don't think we can rule that out. Anything is possible." I finished my cigarette and tossed the remainder into the fire. "Let's all get some rest. We need to put some miles behind us in the morning. Pierce, you're on watch. Wake me up in three hours." I removed my web belt, placed it next to my pack, then laid down on my makeshift mattress of grain sacks. It wasn't the most comfortable of beds, but anything was better than lying on the cold cobblestone floor of the tower.

The night passed uneventfully and relinquished its dark hold on the world to that silent pre-dawn light. Before the sun had even broken the horizon, we were loaded up and on the road heading north out of the charred village. Since Grand-mère Monette forbade April from riding in the cab of the truck with O'Brian, Pierce happily leapt in to save the day and drive the truck for us. April took up position in the shotgun seat to navigate our passage through the winding countryside. I had to laugh. April's little sister Carmen kept looking at me and O'Brian, attempting to mimic her grandmother's burning glare, only to fail and fall apart in small giggling fits.

It wasn't a horrible trip. The road was fairly smooth, not rutted out by heavy military vehicles like some of the roads in the area. Grand-mère Monette sat up with a start at the sound of April's voice when she announced that we'd arrived. The old woman crossed herself and started to pray under her breath. Before the sun had fully broken free of the horizon, we pulled into the dooryard of a well-maintained farmhouse.

Everyone unloaded from the truck and stretched. After I helped the old woman to the ground, she shuffled her way toward the house, beckoning Carmen along, who by that point was locked into what seemed like a life or death staring contest with O'Brian. Grand-mère Monette picked up a rock, hissed, then threw it at the Irishman, breaking his concentration. Even though I couldn't understand what Carmen said, I'm pretty sure she skipped away mocking him. She took her grandmother's hand, then turned to look back to me as they walked away, and in a very heartfelt tone, said thank you.

That right there was enough to brighten anyone's day. I watched after the pair as they walked right through the unlocked front door. April rushed along behind them, muttering something in French. She gathered an armload of wood from the side of the porch and carried it inside, closing the door behind her.

At the very least, it was a picturesque scene deserving of a postcard. The land was beautifully green in all directions. The landscape looked flat and nearly even, with a slight downhill slope that easily stretched out a few hundred feet toward the west. Just off to the side of the house stood a large barn and a number of other outbuildings clad in rough-cut planks of hardwood that had grayed with age. Dirty gray sheep baa'd and milled about under a stand of hardwoods in the fenced-off area behind the barn.

O'Brian walked up beside me, offering me a piece of dried meat from the night before.

"Beautiful, don't you think? As dark as some of the soil is here, I bet crops would thrive," I said as I took the offered meat.

"Aye, it is. But you'd not catch me ever farming this land," the Irishman said between open-mouthed chews.

"Why's that?" I slowly chewed on the piece of dried beef.

O'Brian scoffed then turned to me with a perplexed stare. "You've never raised sheep before, have you, Sergeant?"

"No, I haven't," I said, tearing another bite from the hunk of meat. "We always had a fair number of chickens, a few hogs, and at least one cow for milk, but never any sheep."

"What about your land? Your people never raised large herds of cattle? I thought America was covered in cattle."

I laughed at the realization of what he was saying. "Oh, no. Nothing like what you might see in the movies. Out west they might drive herds like that, but not in Northwest Georgia. My family grew mostly corn, cotton, and tobacco anywhere we could drop seeds into the ground. Paw would keep a close eye on the signs every year before he decided what the main crop would end up being. Some years he'd only plant one or another, but that mainly depended on the demand at market, too. I remember one year we nearly lost everything because of a drought. We could barely haul enough water from the river to grow enough food for ourselves that year."

"That makes a world of sense then," O'Brian said knowingly. "Ya see, lad, most folks on this side of the pond were raised doing one thing their whole lives. They follow in their father's footsteps, who followed in their father's, and so on and so forth. So if there are sheep here at this farm now, there have most likely been sheep on this land for generations. After generations of livestock feeding and trampling the earth, it becomes so compacted that it's hard as a rock. It would take you years of hard work before the land could be easily worked. I don't know about you, but I'd personally choose the route of the least amount of work."

I stared at the Irishman and smiled. My mind spun with thoughts. "I've got an idea…"

Chapter 10

After making sure April and her family were settled, the three of us climbed into the cab of the truck, and drove nonstop back to Chappelle Airfield, each of us taking a turn at the wheel. Overall it wasn't a bad trip. It took us a few hours of navigating around the heavily rutted and blocked routes, or where the engineering corps had blown a bridge to hinder German movements across the countryside. Once we'd made it back to the airfield, I jumped down from the truck before O'Brian had come to a full stop, then turned back to O'Brian and Pierce.

"Hold off on unloading anything just yet. Let me talk to the LT first." I sprinted for the tent to find Lieutenant Rustay sitting behind a field desk, reviewing a stack of reports. He looked up at me with an aggravated glance.

"Sullivan, you finally made it. I was starting to wonder if we should send out a search party to look for you three. We haven't unloaded the trucks yet. I decided to leave that up to you, since I didn't know how you'd like to inventory all the aircraft parts. Grabowski was able to acquire another tent for us, to use as a machine shop or what have you." Rustay glanced up and caught me craning my neck to glance at the reports scattered across the small field desk. His cheeks puffed as he let out an exasperated breath, then he handed me one of the reports. "What do you make of that?" He leaned back in his chair and stretched. He pulled a cigar from his shirt pocket and lit it as I read over the report.

United States Army Field Headquarters
Chippelle Airfield, Chippelle, France, June 29th, 1944

Official report

From: The office of Colonel Archer, Task Force 13

Authorized eyes only

Subject: Eyewitness testimony, Field Report of U.S. Army Staff Sergeant Jim Ellis of the 371st Engineer Construction Battalion, Charlie Company, Scout Detachment Able.

Transcribed from the taped recording of Staff Sergeant Jim Ellis

Date of occurrence: June 25th, 1944

Occurrence Location: South of Caen, France, Orne River crossing, near the village of Brieux

It's with complete shock and astonishment I make this report. I know I'm not suffering from battle fatigue, since the four other members of my team saw what I did and can attest to same.

Our team had been sent well ahead of any of our armored forces, to assess the conditions of bridges along the Orne River, and to systematically destroy a good number of them in order to bottleneck and slow the advance of German forces. We arrived at this particular river crossing in the early afternoon, and had spotted a line of British Cromwell tanks, and a number of those smaller German Panzer 1s. You could see where they'd taken shots at each other; they even scored a number of hits. We could see where shells had struck and exploded on both the British and the German units. Then we noticed these unexplained gashes in the armor, like something had clawed at the tanks, trying to get inside them. One of the tanks had a chunk of its turret removed, like something had just carved into the side of it and tore it away.

The most disturbing part of what we walked into there was the bodies—or really, the lack of bodies. We found bits and pieces of those poor bastards scattered all over the place, inside and outside the tanks. Parts of hands or legs. Jonsie, see, he found the side of this one Kraut's head, still wearing his cap, and it had been *chewed* on. All the parts we saw looked like that. Like a bear or something had gnawed on them. We never did find any fully intact bodies, though. No sign of them, or even any footprints, like the survivors had run away. But there weren't any actual bodies, just parts. Like whatever it was that did it had gotten a full belly or gotten bored with them.

We did find something strange alongside the tanks. It looked like an overgrown jackrabbit, but like it was sick or rabid, maybe. In all my years of hunting, I've never seen anything like it. The rows of nasty, needle-like teeth and these dark gray claws. We bagged it up and brought it back with us because we figured no one would believe us without proof. I passed it off to the colonel's secretary after we got done with the report.

I'm sure when I looked up at Lieutenant Rustay, my eyes were as big as saucers.

"Sounds familiar, doesn't it?" He unfolded a map of the area over the small field desk.

"You can say that again," I said as I looked at the map to get my bearings. "South of Caen, he said." My finger traced across the map, looking for the village of Brieux along the Orne River. I easily spotted it. "That's only a few miles south of where you guys found me at Air Base Jackson. What do you think it means, LT?"

"If these guys ran into them there, and you were here," he said pointing at the map, "we've followed their trail through these villages." Using a pencil, he lightly sketched a line across the face of the map from Brieux that went north to the airfield and stopped at the village of Cristot.

"That's assuming they're the same creatures," I said, coming around to stand next to him instead of looking at an upside-down map.

"It could be a migration," he said questioningly.

"Or something drove them out in the south, and they keep getting pushed north." I paused in thought for a moment; examining the map, I straightened and looked back to the LT. "April's grandmother said something about them. She called them the Pouque, some old legend or something. She said the war disturbed their slumber, and they're angry with the noise of man."

"Well, from what Colonel Archer has told me, the old myths may not be exact, but they *are* at least based in truth. Ancient creatures lurk in dark places. So there's a pretty good chance her grandmother is right about them. Did you get them safely to where they wanted to go?" He started to fold the map, but I stopped him, flattening it back out.

"That's actually part of the reason I'm in here. I found the area where April's family farm should be, just north of Cristot. We dropped them off right about here," I said, pointing. "The land is nearly flat, and solid. Not like here. This area was most likely tilled last season. April's family are sheep herders. The land hasn't been turned in decades at the least. *Jumpin' Jess* could easily take off and land from these fields without any real worries of sinking. Not to mention there's a large barn and other outbuildings already on the site. It would make a perfect place for a forward airbase."

He leaned back in his chair and crossed his arms. "We can't just go barging our way onto someone's land. We wouldn't be any better than the Germans if we did that."

"I've already brought this up with April and her grandmother. They welcomed the idea of hosting us on their land. Well, except for O'Brian. She doesn't trust him because he's Irish, but I told her he was part of the deal. She agreed reluctantly and was otherwise welcoming of the idea. And really, LT, with the mud and rain here on an airfield with almost constant transport traffic, it's only going to get worse for us. *Jess* has a big heavy ass, and it won't get any better. She's really just too heavy for this airfield."

Lieutenant Rustay laced his fingers together and sat quietly in thought for a moment before sucking in a quick breath. "What do they want in exchange for letting us use their land and barn?"

"Nothing more than our protection, sir. Though they did get a little upset with me when I suggested we could rent the barn and use of the field from them. They adamantly refused the offer of payment. The grandmother offered it as a thank you for saving them from the creatures and escorting them home."

Rustay chewed on the end of the cigar as he thought. "And you think the ground is good the way it is? We won't need any heavy equipment, or have to do anything other than to launch and recover?"

"Eventually, maybe," I said honestly. "But for now, no. You could bring in fully loaded B-17s on that ground, and they'd be perfectly fine. Then there's another thing to think about. On top of it all, we'll be close to the last known area of incursion by the creatures. Might make it that much easier to track them down from there, versus here."

He nodded and took a long draw from the cigar, letting a thick cloud of smoke linger about in front of his face, before he blew out a lungful. "Hollywood!"

A moment later Hollywood appeared, pushing his way past the tent flap. He stood at attention and saluted the LT.

"Are you brain-dead, Hollywood?"

"Sir?"

"You don't salute in the field, Private."

"Sorry, sir. It won't happen again, sir," he said, saluting.

"Put your hand down, Hollywood," Rustay said with a long sigh. He slowly rubbed at his temples.

"Shit, sorry, sir." He dropped his hand and tucked it close to his side.

"Forget it, private. Where are you on setting up that new tent?"

"The tent is all set up, sir. We unloaded the trucks then built the tent around them. Figured we should get those engines under cover before it rained or something."

I let out a slight chuckle then bit my knuckle to suppress an all-out fit of laughter. In the short time that I'd had to get to know Hollywood, I knew that he wasn't stupid. But that really said something about the man's character. He had gone above and beyond the call of duty and the orders of his superiors, which I assumed meant that underneath it all, he was a brown-nosing weasel. A complete kiss ass. The kind of guy that would sell you out in the slightest of ways to make himself look good in the eyes of his superiors. I'd have to pay attention and not let my guard down around him.

"Well, I have another task for you. Get with Grabowski and start packing up camp."

"Sir?" Hollywood looked between the two of us, confused.

"Sullivan, when we're done here, go let Pierce know that I want him to requisition those trucks again. I'll fill out a requisition for fuel and ammo to get ourselves established," the LT said, then turned back to Hollywood. "Did I stutter, private? Pack it up, all of it. We're moving our base of operations to a new location that can better support our mission."

"But, sir, we just got it all unloaded."

"It'll be alright private. It'll be good practice for you. Just think of it as on the job training."

"But sir…"

"Dismissed, private!"

"Sir, yes sir," he said, then saluted again.

"Get out, Hollywood!"

"Yes, sir!" The private stumbled over his own two feet as he ran out through the tent flap.

I looked back to the LT with a knowing glare. "I missed something, didn't I?"

"Not really. I caught Hollywood trying to skip out of setting up camp. His overexuberance bit him in the ass just a tad bit."

I laughed. "Yeah, I'd say so." I saluted the lieutenant sarcastically. "Sir!" I laughed. "Let me get out here and give them a hand. The sooner we get packed up, the better."

"Agreed," the LT said amid a cloud of smoke.

Chapter 11

It didn't take us long to get everything packed up and moved to the new location on April's family's farm. We still had a few hours of daylight to set up, since the sun hung a bit above the horizon. The place was alive with motion almost immediately, once we'd pulled in and went to work.

The large barn on the property would be used to store any perishables or equipment we didn't want to chance getting wet in the tents we'd brought with us. One tent would be erected and used as our field command tent. The other one would be used as storage and additional sleeping space, for those who didn't want to sleep in the hayloft of the barn.

We were greeted by April, who escorted her grandmother out to look us over. The old woman smiled and waved at the lot of us as we ran about, setting up camp. I drove the first stake for the command tent in the space between the house and the barn, and set the second corner, then passed off the mallet to Grabowski. The old woman's smile exploded in a wrinkly-faced, toothless grin that only a grandmother can do as I approached the pair. Just moments before she'd been hissing and what I guess was cursing at O'Brian, our Irish explosives expert. April's little sister Carmen ran out and leapt up into my arms, and hugged my neck profusely. She kept repeating something in French, her voice muffled as she buried her face into my shoulder. I turned to April and shook my head.

"She's happy you came back," April said with a slight giggle. "She's saying she won't be afraid to go to sleep if all of you are here. And especially since *you* are back."

April flashed a wry smile that she hid behind her hand. Grand-mère Monette said something while nodding her head slowly. She beamed up at me, but then it turned into a wary glare. April let out a laugh.

"My grandmother does bring up a good point," April said. "Since Carmen has taken a liking to you and will be of marriageable age in a few years, my grandmother would like to know what you are willing to offer as a bride price in exchange for the promise of her hand?"

"Wait, what?" A confounded sigh escaped my lips. I froze and stared back at the two women. Carmen leaned up, still clinging to my neck, and smiled, then said something in French and planted a gentle kiss on my cheek. I dropped the girl to the ground, prying her arms loose from my neck, and took a step backward. "Now hold one damned second."

The old woman coughed and wheezed between cackling breaths, repeatedly slapping her knee. April's shoulders shook with restrained laughter. I could see a tear escape the corner of her eye as she held one hand across her mouth and the other across her stomach.

Carmen stood in front of me, rocking on her heels with her hands innocently behind her back, and said something to me in French.

"Oh," April and Grand-mère Monette both said with surprise, then exploded in all-out uncontrollable laughter.

I watched the three of them with a wary eye. "What did she say?"

After a few moments, April caught her breath and composed herself. "She said," she began, then cleared her throat, stifling a laugh. "She said even though we may have been playing a teeny tiny prank on you," she pinched her finger and thumb together in my direction, "she was absolutely serious about the matter. You look like a capable and kind man, and one is never too young to begin planning for her future."

I looked back down at the young girl, whose smile radiated happiness. She nodded, then hurriedly leapt forward, wrapping her arms around me in an imprisoning embrace.

The two women exploded in laughter once again, then stopped suddenly at the sound of roaring aircraft engines approaching from the north.

I pried the child free from my torso and passed her to April. I started to shake a scolding finger at her, but then decided against it. "She's not serious, is she?"

"I'm afraid she is," April said with a laugh as she stroked Carmen's hair. The girl glared at me, then buried her face in April's bosom.

I watched the sky as *Jumpin' Jess* roared overhead and banked hard, turning back to the northeast. Pierce began a long, circular flight path around the farm and field. I figured he was probably just getting his bearings and a lay of the land. The large fighter aircraft loomed in the distance like a shadowy apparition about to pounce on its prey. We all quietly watched as *Jess* lazily circled around to the field to the south, then once again banked hard, turning back toward the north. With practiced ease, Pierce guided the large black metal bird into line with our newly designated airfield. *Jess* roared by at no more than a hundred feet off the deck as Pierce tested the approach. He must have pushed the throttles to full military power, because as he flew over the field, I could hear the twin Pratt & Whitney R-2800 Double Wasp radial engines power up. The large night fighter suddenly rolled to the right and banked hard, heading back toward the south.

"We can straighten this out later," I said as I turned back to April, pulling my eyes away from *Jess's* sexy dark lines. Pierce began running her through a series of maneuvers while coming around for another approach. "I need to get things ready to catch *Jess.* Y'all stay back near to the house or the barn until I get them parked. And whatever you do, don't just come running out to the plane, especially with the engines running. There're all kinds of things that might hurt or kill you if you get too close. We wouldn't want you to accidentally walk into one of the props. It isn't a pretty sight, trust me."

April pulled Carmen closer as if to protect her from the evil black machine before it could approach them. Pierce passed over the field once more, waggling his wings side to side as he passed by. We could all see him wave from the cockpit window. I retrieved two pairs of wheel chocks from the back of one of the trucks. Slinging the yellow-painted wood blocks over each of my shoulders, I let them dangle by their ropes down my back. I looked over the area in front of the barn. It was fairly well open, no trees or obstacles on this side of the buildings. I stomped on the ground with the heel of my boot, testing the hardness.

"This should do nicely," I mumbled to myself, then dropped a pair of chocks where I stood. We were maybe a hundred feet away from both the house and barn, to allow plenty of room to turn the plane. Then I stepped to my right and dropped the other pair of chocks twenty or so feet away from the first pair.

With little effort, Pierce guided the night fighter gently to the ground and slowly puttered in my direction. I held my hands up over my head and flagged him. As soon as I could see his thumbs up reply, I began to marshal him toward the spot where I wanted him to park. Once in place, I crossed my forearms in front of me and motioned for all stop. Pierce chopped the throttles as he rolled into place and stepped on the brakes.

I ran around to the side and underneath to place the chocks around both of the main landing gear wheels as the engines spit and sputtered to a stop. With a quick push of the latch releases, I popped open the access hatch to the radar operator's station at the rear of the crew compartment. As I lowered the door to hang, I glanced up to see Private Kenny Doyle sitting in the radar operator's position. I swear his head was about to split in half with the ear to ear grin he had. I don't think his smile could have gotten any bigger.

"Did you have a good flight?"

"Absolutely!" He fumbled with the latch of the restraints. "When can I go again?"

"I'll have to make sure you're certified before any combat missions, if that's what you want," I said.

"Wait, can I train on the gunner's position?"

"I don't see why not," I said. "We're a small unit, and everyone needs to know how to fill the positions, if it comes down to it. I honestly don't give a shit whether you're an officer or not. An enlisted grunt can run the radar and turret just as good as any officer."

Doyle let out a giddy squeal. "Sign me up, Sarge!"

"Well, come on down. We've got lots to get done before dark. Go give Grabowski and Hollywood a hand with the command tent. You can stow your gear in the barn for now."

"Will do, Sarge," Doyle said, then tossed his over-stuffed rucksack at the hatch opening, where it lodged itself in place. He stomped on the pack three times before it ripped and finally fell through the hole. I left him to climb out on his own and began the post-flight inspection. Walking around under the right-wing, I checked for leaks and missing fasteners before spotting Pierce. The Marine warrant officer had already climbed out of the cockpit and was looking over the top of the aircraft.

"You were having yourself a little fun up there, weren't you?"

Pierce jumped with a start at the sound of my voice, then looked down in my direction. "Don't do that to me. You trying to give me a heart attack?" He took a calming breath. "What did you say?"

"I said, were you having fun up there? Cause it sure looked like it from the ground, with the way you were running *Jess* through her paces."

"Oh, that," Pierce said. "Yeah, this plane is a beast. I didn't think a plane this big could maneuver as well as she does. And I've never flown an aircraft with those spoiler-type ailerons before. They feel weird, but she handles so much easier at low speeds with them."

"Doyle looked like he was thoroughly enjoying himself," I said. "He's interested in flight crew training."

A surprised look crossed Pierce's face. "We can train him, but until he's been under fire in combat, we won't know if he'll be good or not."

"That's fair enough," I said. "And training up a few others to fill in if I have to be somewhere else isn't going to hurt us any."

"Sergeant," April said softly. We both turned to look in the direction of her voice to find all three of the Chevrolet women looking at the aircraft in wonderment. She looked upward at Pierce with a glowing smile, then quickly waved at him with a roll of her fingers.

He waved back, then slid his hands into his pockets and nervously rocked on his heels. "Ladies," he said with an awkward nod, then turned back to me with a pleading look.

"How about you go ahead and knock out the top inspection while you're up there," I said, trying to save the young Marine from his own self-imposed discomfort.

"Yeah, sure, that's a great idea," he said. "I need to learn every curve and line of her airframe anyway, right?" His eyes drifted back to April. She immediately looked away as her neck and ears flushed a bright shade of red.

I caught a glimpse from the corner of my eye of Grand-mère Monette as she shot a narrow-eyed glare up at the young pilot.

"Have any of you lovely ladies ever seen an aircraft up close before?" I asked, trying to save Pierce from total disaster.

April said something to the other two in French, then looked back to me. "No, we have not."

"Well, then, you're in for a treat," I said. "This is the P-61, called the Black Widow," I said, reciting a line from a training video. I motioned at the large black aircraft. "She's well named, because she packs four .50 caliber machine guns and four 20mm cannons. An obituary notice goes with each bite...."

Chapter 12

By the end of the following week, we'd more or less gotten the camp set up. After a bit of back and forth discussion, and a few well-founded concerns surrounding the gremlins, we decided against bunking in the tents. In nearly no time at all, we completely converted the hayloft of the barn into a barracks, where there'd be something more than a thin layer of canvas to protect us from the elements and the gremlin hordes if they happened to come back our way. We'd designated the lower area of the barn as our communal living and work area, while the tents served as storage for parts and supplies.

Pierce and O'Brian had been instrumental in helping me rearm *Jess*. With the help of Lieutenant Rustay, O'Brian had managed to acquire several empty drop tanks and a fair selection of tools while on a supply run back to Chippelle Airfield. The little Irishman had a knack for metal fabrication I couldn't even come close to matching. He'd also taken a truck back to Air Base Jackson to salvage sheet metal from the remains of my previous unit. The external fuel tanks were perfect for the plan O'Brian and I had come up with for modifications to *Jumpin' Jess*.

Originally intended to mount under the wings of the German Messerschmitt BF 110 heavy fighters that had been stationed at Chippelle Airfield before the invasion of Normandy, two of the nine-hundred-liter fuel tanks would be used instead as gun pods, modified as needed to internally mount a 20mm cannon and two additional .50 caliber Browning M2 machine guns, along with their respective ammo, which would be mounted to the outer munitions mount points on the wings, and controlled by the pilot. As for the smaller three-hundred-liter fuel tanks they'd found, we planned to convert them for use as incendiary bombs that could be attached to multi-point racks mounted beneath each wing at factory mount points just outboard of the engine nacelles.

We hadn't quite finished the modifications for *Jess* when the LT returned from a separate supply run to Chippelle Airfield. Besides our standard allotment of ammo, rations, and other necessities, he'd brought back an entire fuel truck filled to the brim with high-grade aircraft fuel, and our first regular assignment. It didn't have anything to do with the gremlin menace roaming the French countryside, but it still fell into the realm of strange, and as such, landed smack dab in our laps. Apparently there had been a number of aircraft lost in an area north of Paris, as aircrews returned from missions deep behind enemy lines during the hours surrounding dawn. This inconvenience had led to the rerouting of allied aircraft returning from missions, causing their aircrews to stretch their already precious fuel reserves even more so on an already long trip into enemy airspace.

Since we had the only radar-equipped aircraft not currently dedicated to a vital mission, our orders were to patrol the area with caution, identify the threat, and eliminate that threat if at all possible. If we couldn't accomplish the mission with our currently assigned equipment, we were to retreat with the information, and call in the necessary reinforcements to complete the mission.

Since I was the only member of our team currently qualified to operate the radar aboard *Jess*, I was assigned as the mission RO, or Radar Operator, this go around. Pierce, of course, would be on the mission, since he was our one and only pilot, but we still needed someone in the gunner's seat. After a brief discussion between myself, Pierce, and the LT, it was decided that this would be the perfect mission to begin Private Doyle's training and qualification on the General Electric Central Station Fire Control System utilized onboard the P-61 aircraft.

Being that he was the lowest-ranking member of the mission, I sent Doyle to snag a few ration packs for each of us, then bring the fuel truck over while I began the preflight inspection. Since we'd be out on patrol for a few hours, I packed away a ration pack at each of our stations. In no time flat, I had *Jess* serviced, loaded, and ready to roll, while Pierce worked out our flight plan.

Each of us hit the sack and caught at least a few hours of restless shuteye in the intervening hours before our departure. Somewhere around 0300 I kicked at Doyle's boot as I passed by, heading for the ladder that led up to the hayloft.

"Time to get up and at 'em if you want to be a hero, Private," I said in a whispered tone to keep from waking anyone else. Sleep was one of the precious commodities you could never get enough of on the battlefield. There always seemed to be something to do or somewhere to go that always interrupted the precious few solid hours you did manage to get.

Doyle scrambled to his feet. Groggily grabbing for his jacket and the rucksack he had been using as a pillow, he suddenly froze. "I... I don't know, Sarge," he stammered, then nervously set his pack down and donned his field coat in preparation for the high altitude flight like I had instructed him.

"Don't know about what, Doyle?"

"I... I...," he said, taking a deep, frustrated breath.

"Come on now, spit it out," I said. "We only have a limited amount of time to get ourselves into position, Private."

"I don't know about flying. I mean, I've flown without a problem, but there's a good chance we might get shot out of the sky, isn't there?"

"Well, yeah," I said, quietly nodding my head. "There's always a chance of getting shot down any time we're airborne. Ya know, I heard this rumor there's a war on," I said jokingly, cupping my hand to my mouth as if passing a secret.

"B... but, you aren't scared?"

"Why, hell yeah, I'm scared." I patted him on the shoulder. "In all honesty, I'm scared shitless. But ya see, if we don't do the missions we're assigned, that might leave a hole open for a Jerry to slip through that could hurt or even kill someone that I love and care about. So, I suck it up and do the job."

"Suck it up and do the job," he repeated in a low tone to himself. He stared off into space as he repeated the words and slung his pack over his shoulders, then turned back to me. "Alright. Let's do this." He nodded and practically leapt down the wooden ladder.

In short order, we were cranked and airborne, heading nearly due east on a direct course for Reims. Once we'd been in flight for a predetermined amount of time, Pierce planned to begin a search pattern by turning north and dividing the countryside into a search grid. This would allow us to utilize *Jess's* SCR-720 radar to its max range of nearly five miles, covering the most area in the shortest amount of time.

With *Jess's* impressive maximum airspeed of 366 mph, we crossed the distance to our first navigation point in about thirty minutes once we were aloft. The skies were littered with scattered puffy cumulus clouds high up in the atmosphere, with the moon shining bright, even though it was well past its three-quarter full waxing gibbous phase. Pierce lightly hummed and whistled a happy tune to himself in a hushed, under the breath tone.

If not for the crew headset I wore, I'd be completely ignorant of anything else going on aboard the aircraft. The RO's position aboard the P-61 was a lonely one. You entered the rear crew compartment from an underslung hatch and were totally isolated from the pilot and gunner, who were positioned forward of the aircraft's quad-mounted .50 caliber M2 turret. If you weren't staring at the dual radar readouts, the secondary gunner's sighting system, or a myriad of other instruments, you could turn around and stare out the plexiglass bubble dome at the rear of the crew gondola and watch the world race by below. Pierce's humming became slightly louder as we banked, turning back toward the east for the next leg of our search pattern.

We continued this pattern for some time in the dark hours before dawn. Before too long we could see the threat of morning glowing on the eastern horizon.

The comms crackled with the sound of someone fiddling with the mouthpiece. "What's up with you, Pierce?" Doyle asked in an almost annoyed tone. "We're out here on a combat mission, and you're acting like it's the best day of your life."

"Well, maybe it is, Private." Pierce blew out into the mic. "What business is it of yours?"

I laughed at Pierce's biting question. "Don't let him get to you, Doyle. Ya see, my guess is he really isn't here with us at all right now. His head is floating about way up there in the clouds, daydreaming about April."

"You think so, do you?" Pierce jeered.

"I know so," I said. "And I bet before we set off on this little mission, he even managed to steal a kiss. A dame like that isn't going to have anything to do with a guy like me."

Pierce blew out another frustrated breath. "You have *got* to be out of your mind, you know that?" Annoyingly loud tongue clicks suddenly reverberated through the headset.

"Could you please stop that," Doyle said loudly. "I can hear you clicking without the headset."

"He's just upset that I'm right," I said. "I saw the two of you sneak away around the side of the barn before we loaded up. So is a French kiss from a French woman as good as they make it out to be?"

"You'd better mind your own business if you know what's good for you, Sullivan," Pierce threatened.

"Can we please talk about something else?" Doyle said, interrupting.

"Why?" I goaded. "What's wrong, Private? Don't like girls or something?"

"Oh no, nothing like that," Doyle hurriedly said. "I'd just rather Pierce kept himself focused on flying rather than arguing."

"Now, see, that's not how this works, Private," I said with a laugh.

Pierce chuckled, then added, "He's right, Private. You just opened a can of worms you probably didn't want to."

"Come on, Doyle," I coaxed. "We've barely heard anything about you yet. Where are you from, what did you do before the war? Is there a girl waiting on you back home?"

"She must be pretty dog ugly if she's waiting around for him, wouldn't you say, Sarge?" Pierce said, laughing.

"Hey, now! I'm not that ugly! Am I, Sarge?"

"Well, maybe ugly *is* a bit harsh there, Pierce," I said.

"Alright, alright, maybe you're right, Sarge," Pierce said. "I take back the ugly comment. I'd say you're more of the homely type." Pierce let out a loud donkey chuckle that I could hear over the engines from the rear compartment.

"Don't listen to him, Doyle," I said. "He's just jealous that he doesn't have someone waiting on him. Seriously though, Doyle. You got someone waiting on you back home?"

"Nah... not really," the private said reluctantly. "There were a few I'd talk to every now and then, but nothing really serious. I really didn't have time for girls before the war."

"Wait? What?" Pierce burst out in laughter. "Did I just hear you right? No time for girls? You can't be serious,

Doyle. That's crazy talk. The next thing you know, you'll be chanting 'Heil Hitler'."

"No... I'm serious," Doyle stuttered. "I was so focused on my photography career that I just didn't have time to date. I'd been trying for well over a year to get into *The Nashville Tennessean* before I was drafted."

"I've seen that rag before," I said. "Every now and then someone would leave a copy they'd brought with them in the lobby of the Read House in Chattanooga when I worked there. So, you got anything published yet?"

"Well, no. Not yet." Regret hung heavy in Doyle's words.

"So, then, what gives?" Pierce prodded. "Aren't you good enough for them or something?"

Doyle let out a heavy sigh. "I honestly don't know. I submit my photos and the stories behind them, but they never get published, and I never get any feedback. It's rare that I ever see the pictures again. I don't know if it's my photo style, or maybe something wrong with my writing style."

Honest curiosity had started to set in when a thought suddenly struck me. "How do you sign the stories?"

"What do you mean?"

"What name do you use?"

"Oh, I use my name," Doyle said, sounding confused. "Why?"

"Because the problem could just be as simple as using a pen name," I said. "A lot of people still don't trust the

Irish, let alone want to read anything they have to say about something, and your name just happens to be Doyle. A true and proper Irish name if I've ever heard one. I've known more than a few good Irish families back in Walker County."

"You know," Doyle said, "I never thought about that before. You could be right."

A pattern of lines suddenly appeared on the radar displays. I adjusted the receiver gain control, bringing the pattern into focus, then adjusted the range control. The pattern unfocused just as soon as I got it into focus, so I adjusted the range control again, bringing it into a tighter pattern, then trimmed the focus control. Again the pattern blurred just as soon as I got it cleaned up.

"Look, alive ladies," I shouted into the mouthpiece. "I'm picking up a bogie on the radar, and it's moving fast. *Really* fast..."

"How fast?" Pierce excitedly asked.

"It's closing the miles with us just as soon as I adjust the readout," I replied, dumbfounded by the display. "Do you see the indicator on your screen, Pierce?"

"Yeah, I see it, but I don't know what I'm looking at. Are you sure you're reading that right? It's got to be wrong. There's nothing in the inventory that can move that fast."

"What about the Germans?" Doyle asked. "Could they have something that can move that fast?"

The constant growling roar of *Jess's* Double Wasp engines were briefly and abruptly drowned out by a high-pitched scream of something mechanical as it blew by us in the opposite direction.

"Holy shit!" Pierce shouted over the headset, then *Jess* suddenly banked hard to the right. "I guess there *is* something that can move that fast!"

"What was that?" Doyle sounded nervous and shaken.

"I don't know," I said. "Just get the guns warmed up like I showed you. That thing that just flew by us sounded entirely too angry to be one of ours. I've never heard anything that sounded like that before."

We could still hear the rumble of the thing in the distance as it circled opposite of us. All three of us scanned the dark skies outside our crew compartments for any glimpse of the aircraft that chewed up the sky.

"I see something!" Doyle shouted, followed by the unmistakable *tat, tat, tat* of the quad M2 Browning machine guns that roared to life above my head. I looked in the direction the tracer rounds flew and saw nothing in the sky above.

"Stand down, Doyle," I shouted into the headset mouthpiece.

"What the hell is wrong with you, Private? We're not even in range, and you just gave away our position! Both of you hang on tight!"

Jess suddenly rolled, and the large fighter dove, falling backward from the sky only to jink back to the west as

Pierce brought her nose high. We accelerated upward, and the pitch of the engines changed, as I assumed Pierce had shoved the throttles forward to full power.

I looked back to my still blank displays, then scanned the slowly brightening sky.

"There! Behind us and coming quick!" I'd barely gotten the words out when *Jess* suddenly shook. Multiple impacts struck the airframe as the thing shot past us like a streak of lighting. I could just make out the shape of the craft before it became too hard to see. It looked to be about the size of a small fighter with an engine nacelle mounted beneath each of its low-slung wings. Pierce maneuvered *Jess* upward, aiming our nose in the direction of the aircraft. Our four 20mm cannons lit up the sky. Tracers danced in the air around the faint shape as it faded from view.

"You ever saw anything like that before?" Pierce asked.

"Never," I replied, then turned back to my displays, to find that the patterns had returned. I adjusted the settings, hoping to see the enemy aircraft without actually seeing him. "Start banking to the right and nose down a little," I said, guiding Pierce into position. "You can see the angle of attack on your display."

"I see it," Pierce said.

"Doyle, get ready," I said. "He's coming in hot and on a straight line for us."

"Roger that," Doyle said.

"There! That's it, you're lined up, Pierce! Fire!" I ordered.

I felt the vibration of the 20mm cannons course through *Jess's* frame in time to the great thundering roar that accompanied them as the rounds flew forward into the sky ahead of us. I watched through the rear gunner's sights, then saw the enemy appear and disappear from view as it tore through the sky in an angry growl. Rounds raked our left wing as the enemy aircraft raced by. I suddenly heard an odd mechanical *shink, shink, shink* over the headset.

"That doesn't sound right," Pierce said over the comms. "What the hell are you doing, Private? You're supposed to shoot the enemy with the guns, not a camera!"

"Sorry," Doyle said. "I couldn't resist."

"Dammit, Doyle! Shoot the damn thing," I ordered.

Pierce rolled us upside down and executed another backward dive. The engines screamed from the added airspeed of the dive as we corkscrewed, then banked hard to the left and nose high, trying to get behind the enemy aircraft. I saw the distinctive glint of early morning sunlight across his windscreen as we banked and jinked.

"He's still behind us!"

We banked up and right, pulling an acrobatic u-turn, then rolled upright on an intercept course with the enemy aircraft. The cannons exploded to life once again with intermittent bursts.

"This guy is too nimble," Pierce shouted over the noise of the 20mm guns. "I can't get a bead on him."

Sparks erupted from the radio transmitter mounted to the bulkhead in front of me, and three large holes appeared in the side of the compartment.

"What the hell are you doing up there? You're going to get us shot down!"

Jess rolled over onto her back and shook violently. She porpoised in a sudden surge of negative Gs and began a slow fall from heaven. One of the engines suddenly began to spit and sputter as the screaming roar of our hardnosed dive grew louder. Black smoke billowed out and trailed behind us from our left engine.

"Pierce! Doyle! Do either of you copy me?"

Rounds struck at our tail, and two more penetrated my compartment from the lower left. Switching control of the upper quad turret to the rear gunner's station, I turned to aim, but found the unit failed to respond, acting like it was jammed or locked in place. I flipped the switch multiple times, with the same result. A wave of hopelessness washed over me. I turned, looking aft through the blown plexiglass dome at the rear of the compartment, and saw our attacker closing the distance.

In the dim early morning light, I was able to see more of its details. It was a sleek-looking straight-winged craft that bore a striking resemblance to a gray speckled shark stalking its prey. Flashes of light erupted from the nose of the craft, illuminating its sleek form even more, when

I noticed something extremely odd. Nowhere across its form did I see the distinctive blur of rotating propeller blades. Maybe it was just the angle of the sun in relation to our tandem dive. *Jess* began a slow corkscrew left, then side slipped right in a sudden and abrupt jink that tossed me about in my seat. I helplessly watched as the enemy aircraft continued to gain on us in our uncontrolled suicide dive. Tracer rounds danced about, encircling us in a shroud of light. Pieces of sheet metal flapped in the airstream and tore away from the leading edge of the right vertical stabilizer as the enemy's rounds found their target.

By this point, the thick black smoke from the engine had disappeared, and the attacking aircraft was so close I could clearly see the pilot through the rounded dome of the canopy. White iron crosses stood out clearly on the top of both of the aircraft's wings. I looked back at the Luftwaffe pilot, his goggles reflecting the early morning light as he looked up at me from below our centerline. Out of some strange, habitual need, I held up my hand and waved. He popped his right hand up to his brow and lingered there for a moment in a proper salute. As soon as I returned the salute, he dropped his hand and resumed firing.

Jess unexpectedly shuddered as the left engine sputtered back to life amid belches of dark gray smoke. The engine went to full throttle, and we pulled up hard. I could hear the buckling of her sheet metal and wing spars as she absorbed the extreme G forces being exerted across her airframe. We banked left, dumping some of the excess force, then rolled right and slalomed, nosing upward and skyward, gaining altitude.

Blinding white tracer rounds rocketed aft and upward in a nearly solid line of projectiles that led ahead of the German fighter. The enemy pilot jinked his aircraft to the right, but not before the .50 caliber rounds from *Jess's* turret ripped into his left-wing. I watched as the rounds chewed their way inboard, across the leading edge of the wing, before feasting upon the left engine nacelle. Hunks of burning metal darted out in all directions as the left engine exploded, engulfed in orange flames. The tracers continued their inboard march across the wing, eventually removing the small bubble canopy in a detonation of shattered glass. The small fighter swerved left, then nosed down.

In those last few moments that stretched only the span of a few heartbeats, I watched as the German pilot fought with his dying aircraft. He pulled back on the stick with everything he had, just before the left engine exploded, separating the wing from the fuselage. The two sections fell away like meteorites shrouded in a blanket of smoke and flames. I popped a salute to the enemy pilot and rendered my respects just as he had moments before, then wiped away the tears that streamed down my cheeks.

Chapter 13

From the quiet isolation of the radar operator's compartment, I watched the morning landscape come to life as we slowly limped our wounded aircraft back to base. Apparently a round from the German fighter had grazed the side of Pierce's head and momentarily knocked him unconscious, leaving him with a noticeable bald streak down the side of his head. Doyle had managed to shake him awake enough to pull us out of the death dive before his gunnery training returned to Doyle's panicked mind. I'm sure as hell glad he listened. He hit that German fighter just in the nick of time to save our sorry asses.

As soon as we were back on solid ground, I immediately assessed the damage and began repairs. I assigned some of the tasks, like patching holes, to O'Brian, while I worked on the damaged left engine, and Perunko worked on replacing shot up components and the wiring issues, dividing the workload. It didn't take us long before *Jess* was patched up, and we finished the modifications. The new gun pods were installed, bore-sighted, and ready for action. By the middle of the next day, we'd finished our operational checks, and O'Brian had finished mixing his incendiary concoction. He filled the three-hundred-liter German drop tanks, and mounted four of them, one to each of *Jess's* external fuel tank mounts.

By this point in the war, the allied forces had pushed across the French countryside, regaining control of the cities of Saint-Lô and Caen, delivering a crushing blow to the occupying German forces. We'd been seeing a lot more air traffic passing through, heading for what we thought was Paris. From what Lieutenant Rustay had been able to find out from headquarters, it was exactly what we'd been thinking. The battle for Paris had begun. The Allied forces were pushing deeper into enemy territory, giving the Germans hell the entire time.

I was starting to think Grand-mère Monette was right, that these gremlins were angry with man. The more the war progressed and pressed inland, the stranger the reports coming across our desk from headquarters at Chippelle Airfield. Transport convoys attacked by unknown creatures, tanks and artillery pieces shredded, left to rust where they were. I really think there was something to what she'd told us. We've all heard those kinda stories from the old-timers. Some you believe, others you don't. I read through one report after the next, taking in the descriptions of damage to equipment and the remains of soldiers left behind on the scenes. Whatever they were, they didn't have a side in this fight. Or maybe they did. Maybe they had their side, and Grand-mère Monette was right, down to the fact that we'd awakened them from their slumber. It was like believing in stories of the boogeyman, only this particular story was real.

We got an encrypted call over the radio late one afternoon that Hollywood was able to translate using the standard Allied cipher, which meant it wasn't close to top-secret information, but headquarters didn't want to make it stupid easy for the Germans to know what was happening on our side of the lines. Apparently our guys had come across a German equipment convoy blocking a bridge over the river Orne, near the town of La Butte, and it had been overrun by what they described as rabid jackrabbits from hell. They reported the creatures had swarmed over the convoy and the steam engine the Germans had been loading their equipment on to.

Our guys on the ground had called in air support, which arrived in the form of a B-25 Mitchell II from the Royal Air Force's 98th Squadron out of Dunsfold, England. They'd reported that several of the things had leathery, bat-like wings and had attempted to fly high enough to attack the Mitchell II, which was startling news to all of us. The LT relayed a message back to them, taking official command of the situation, and ordered the Mitchell to provide overwatch until we could arrive on site. For the sake of saving their own skins, our guys on the ground kept their distance. They didn't know where to even begin dealing with the creatures. I kind of laughed at that part of the message as Hollywood read it out loud to everyone gathered around the radio in our converted command center.

"That's the easy part," I said. "Use everything you've got, and kill it with fire." More than a few of the guys let out a chuckle.

Considering there wasn't much chance of running into any enemy aircraft on this mission, I decided to send both Grabowski and Hollywood up with Pierce so they could both get some time in *Jess's* gunner seats. Grabowski, being the more technically inclined of the two, asked if he could take the rear radar operator's position so he could play with the radios and radar system as well. "Get a real feel for them," as he put it. So I ran both of them through the basics of the turret's operation and the finer points of the Central Station Fire Control System, then gave them explicit instructions not to break my girl.

After the LT relayed a message that we were en route and would be on-site in just over an hour, I mounted a portable UHF transmitter in the cab of our transport truck, while Doyle, O'Brian, and Perunko loaded up their gear. In short order, we were on the road and heading for La Butte.

Within twenty minutes of launch, Pierce began relaying information back to us. He'd taken up an overwatch position parallel with the RAF B-25 that was on site. The creatures were everywhere, according to our Marine Corps warrant officer. He reported a few survivors, who had taken refuge atop the train and surrounding structures. They'd even taken potshots at the two circling aircraft before becoming dinner for the creatures on the ground.

Being the impatient type, Hollywood had convinced Pierce to let him have a little target practice while they waited for us to arrive. He figured there wasn't anyone left to save on the ground, so it couldn't hurt to take a few of the things out. Using *Jess's* quad .50 caliber turret, Hollywood and Grabowski took turns shredding the creatures. They barely scratched the surface of their numbers, but they at least managed to take out a few of the creatures, and get a feel for the firing system. The Brits even joined in on a little target practice, firing from the lower dustbin turret mounted to the belly of their B-25 Mitchell II. From the sounds of the radio chatter between the two aircraft as we approached, they'd made a game of taking out the greatest number of gremlins in a single shot.

I'd never really had much interaction with any of the British Royal Air Force personnel before, but from the sounds of the radio chatter, they were as competitive as any of us average Joes serving in the United States Armed Forces. At one point, we were starting to wonder if they were going to start firing on each other. The LT had to chime in and break up a heated argument when it sounded like the Brits were trying to pick a fight with Hollywood.

By the time we arrived and met up with the guys on the ground, both aircraft crews had more or less gotten bored with the wholesale slaughter. The area was mostly farmland, and fields for livestock, with the scattered stand of trees or berm-type hedgerows dividing properties. The U.S. Sixth Army Special Reconnaissance Unit, Kilo Squad that had called in the situation had set up a defensive position a little over half a mile away. Even from this distance, and without binoculars, we could see the swarm of creatures within view along the roadway. They moved and seethed about over the train and vehicles, almost like they were one large organism, feasting on the remains of the German battalion.

"Who's in charge here?" Lieutenant Rustay shouted as he leapt from the passenger seat of the truck before I'd even brought the large vehicle to a complete stop.

"I am," a butter bar Army lieutenant said as he wiped the crust from his sleep-deprived eyes. He approached Rustay and held out his hand. "Second Lieutenant Matt Byrd, Sixth Army, Kilo Squad."

"First Lieutenant Craig Rustay," he said, taking the other man's hand to shake. "I've had reports coming in from our eyes in the sky," he said, pointing skyward toward the circling P-61 Black Widow. "Do you have anything new to report from the ground?"

"Not really," Byrd said, scratching at a few days' worth of stubble. "There must have been some supplies or something on one of the train cars. They mostly swarmed over this one boxcar, but otherwise, no, nothing has really changed. They haven't seemed to notice us, or even really care, from what we can tell. But we also haven't gone out of our way to announce our presence here, either."

Lieutenant Rustay shaded his eyes and stared down the roadway at the pack of creatures swarming over the bridge and train car, then turned back to Lieutenant Byrd. "Do you know of any reason the train or any of the other equipment should be saved?"

"Not really," Byrd said. "We aren't even sure who may have been on that convoy fleeing from our boys. Could be anyone, or could be no one of importance."

O'Brian laughed. "Anyone of bloody importance is in one of those thing's bellies by now."

Lieutenant Byrd glanced over at O'Brian. The color of his face washed out to white as the horrific realization of the Irishman's words sank into the young officer's mind.

"Thank you for holding this position for us, Byrd. We can take it from here," Rustay said, then turned back to me. "Get those birds on the horn. Find out if the bomber has any bombs on board."

I climbed back into the cab of the truck and keyed the mic. "RAF bomber, this is Widowmakers Actual, come in."

"We copy you, Widowmakers Actual, this is RAF FV992," a voice with a thick British accent said across the airwaves.

"Ask them if they're carrying a belly full of munitions," Rustay said to me.

"Gotcha, LT," I said, then turned back to the radio and keyed the mic. "What sort of loadout did you fellas leave with?"

The radio popped to life, followed by static. "A full three-thousand-pound complement of Jerry poppers," the faceless voice stated proudly.

Rustay looked upward, tracking the bomber through the air as it passed behind them to the west. "Tell them to have a little fun with target practice. The same goes for Pierce. Let's try out those incendiary bombs you boys rigged up."

Widowmakers

I caught a glimpse of a wide smile crossing O'Brian's face. He ran and clambered onto the hood of the truck to get himself a better view.

"This is Widowmaker Actual. RAF FV992, Widowmaker Zero One, you are cleared to attack at will. I repeat. This is Widowmaker Actual. RAF FV992, Widowmaker Zero One, you are cleared to attack all visible enemy targets. Friendly fire approximately one-half mile to the west of the bridge. Acknowledge."

"Widowmaker Zero One acknowledges," Pierce replied over the radio.

"RAF FV992 acknowledges also," the aristocratic British voice replied.

"You are cleared for weapons hot; happy hunting fellas," I said with a laugh.

"Copy that," both crews replied before lining up on the target.

The big North American B-25 Mitchell medium bomber powered up, and her R-2600 Twin Cyclone engines growled as her three-bladed propellers chewed up the airspace ahead of her. The big, lumbering airplane suddenly banked hard to the left, aligning herself with the path of the river and railroad tracks.

If I had to guess, I'd say she was at maximum speed, only a thousand feet or so off the ground. We watched as she leveled out and flew in straight as an arrow, her bomb bay doors open. Upon releasing her payload, the full complement of bombs fell away as the bomber roared by overhead. We spotted several of the winged gremlins taking flight in pursuit of the attacking aircraft as bombs fell away past them.

Great balls of flame and smoke erupted along the line of the bomber's flight path. Chunks of dirt, equipment, and creatures flew high into the sky. Every one of the spectators perched atop our truck whooped and cheered at the destruction. The B-25 nosed up, its bomb bay doors closed, and the lower dustbin turret began firing into the fray as they continued around and back into the overwatch pattern.

I keyed the mic. "RAF FV992, two bogeys on your tail and climbing slowly. Do you need assistance with them?"

Static buzzed from the radio as it came to life once again.

"Copy that, Widowmaker Actual. We see them. No assistance needed." Machine gun fire from the lower turret was joined by the upper dome turret.

The radio buzzed with static again.

"RAF FV992, this is Widowmaker Zero One. That wasn't a bad looking run, guys," Pierce said over the airwaves. "A perfect, by the book bombing approach." I could hear the challenging sarcastic tone in his voice. "How about you boys just stay back and let a professional show you how it's done?" I looked to the east, where the unmistakable black silhouette of *Jumpin' Jess* stood out against the blue sky. She continued in the circular overwatch pattern, heading north in preparation for her attack run.

The soldiers surrounding me hung on every word coming from the radio. O'Brian looked up at me with wide eyes. "Has the lad ever dropped bombs before?"

Widowmakers

I shrugged my shoulders. "I've honestly got no clue. Guess we're about to find out."

Before the words were out of my mouth, cigarettes, gold coins, and other items of value were placed in the hands of a young private, who offered five to one odds that Warrant Officer Pierce would fail at what they assumed might be his first attempt at a bombing run ever.

I keyed the mic. "Widowmaker Actual to Widowmaker Zero One, come in, over."

"Go ahead, Widowmaker Actual."

"Hey, hotshot, have you ever dropped bombs before?"

"In theory… yes."

The young private suddenly changed the odds from five to one to ten to one that Pierce would fail, and twenty to one odds he would crash on approach.

I keyed the mic again. "So that's a no?"

"Widowmaker Aero One, RAF FV992, would you like me to walk you through the steps of a proper, by the book bombing run?"

"While the offer is very much appreciated, RAF FV992, I have the situation completely under control."

We watched with morbid fascination as the P-61 Black Widow banked hard to the left, aligning itself with the river and railroad tracks. Its Pratt & Whitney radial engines let out what could be called a war cry as Pierce pushed her to full military power and tipped her nose earthward. The midnight black gunship flashed to life as the eight .50 caliber M2 machine guns and the six 20mm cannons belched fire and spewed forth lead at a maddening rate. The cacophony of impacts that followed reverberated over the picturesque landscape on a light summer breeze. The barrage continued as Pierce guided *Jess* down into a cloud of the flying gremlins, their leathery wings flapping furiously to gain altitude and meet the approaching aircraft.

I keyed the mic. "Pull up. You don't want to take one of those things in a prop or one of the engines. It'll be ten times worse than any bird strike, as dense as those things are."

"Don't get yourself bent out of shape," Pierce said over the radio. "I've got the situation completely under control."

"This guy is suicidal," one of the recon guys said out loud to no one in particular.

We all heard the moment O'Brian's four jury-rigged bombs detached from their make-shift wing mounts with a loud snap and began their plummet to earth. *Jess's* nose violently jerked skyward from the sudden loss of over twenty-five hundred pounds of incendiary ambrosia. The subsequent fireball roiled skyward, engulfing *Jess*, her crew, and the world surrounding the large fighter aircraft. Trees immediately burst into flames, gremlins fell from the sky as incinerated ash, and a scorched, smoldering night fighter thundered out from the convulsing fireball it left behind in its wake. The twin engines momentarily spit and sputtered, then roared back to life as they caught their breath and resumed their duty

"Holy shit," one of the soldiers said in awe, muttering to himself.

"I'll second that," another whispered, then awkwardly cleared his throat and held out a hand to the bookie private. "They survived, Ronny, pay up."

"What?" The private looked back at the retreating aircraft. "They got scorched by their own bombs."

"They didn't crash, so it doesn't count," the corporal argued, reaching for a pack of cigarettes in the private's hand.

"Corporal Nowlin is right," another of the recon guys said as he approached the private. "Pay up, Ronny."

Secondary explosions rocked the rail line and bridge. Parts of exploding vehicles soared high above the tree line.

The radio suddenly popped with static.

"Widowmaker Zero One, this is RAF FV992, we think we've picked up a few hitchhikers. Can you confirm?"

"Widowmaker Zero One copies, RAF FV992," Pierce replied over the airwaves. "Lower your airspeed, and we'll come around to you."

"Copy that, Widowmaker Zero One," the thick British voice said.

The sudden pop of gunfire pulled my attention away from the radio chatter of the aircraft above. I looked up to see one of the recon team members standing to the side of the truck as he checked the breech of his M1 Garand, aimed, and fired once more. My eyes automatically trailed along the line the barrel pointed and followed that down the road in the direction of the bridge. Everyone around me must have been following the same line of thought because, at about the same time my eyes locked onto the horde of gremlins swarming down the country roadway, the soldiers surrounding me rushed into a flurry of curses and motion.

I grabbed my own rifle and, leaning on the open passenger door of the truck, I steadied myself, aimed, and fired. At this range of maybe just over two hundred yards, the creatures were barely a tannish-brown blur on the gray line of pavement, but we'd gotten so used to seeing the things, we could make them out even when the distance was in the range of miles.

The creatures rushed across the bridge and covered half the distance in what seemed like a handful of heartbeats. I took my time, breathed, aimed, and squeezed the trigger. The target range portion of boot camp was a piece of cake. I'd spent most of my life with a rifle in hand, hunting deer and boar on the backside of Lookout Mountain. It's one of those things that just becomes natural after a while, especially when that thing means meat on the table and a full belly for a day or two. You tend to get really good at killing things when you learn firsthand what true hunger is like.

Another of the gremlins flew back with a .30 caliber-sized hole in its head. Some of the others did the same, their shots on target, but from what I could tell, most of the shots being fired by the others weren't anywhere near close.

"We need to get out of here," the young private named Ronny shouted as he ran away into the field behind us.

"Bloody fucking worthless Americans," O'Brian grumbled as he dropped his rifle on the hood of the truck and ran rearward over the top of the cab.

The bolt of my M1 locked back, ejecting the clip after I fired the final round. I reached back into an ammo pouch on my belt, grabbed a fresh clip, slid it home, and closed the breech.

Another of the recon guys broke away from our firing line, fear overtaking him as the swarm of gremlins continued their headlong charge in our direction. I fired again, taking down another of the creatures before the urge to run screamed in the back of my mind.

"LT," I shouted, "what's the plan?"

"Fall back!" Lieutenant Rustay stepped backward, fired, then turned to run, and stopped in his tracks as a stream of liquid fire shot down the roadway, painting its surface in a viscous, burning hell.

"Bloody fucking worthless Americans!" O'Brian shouted, appearing as if out of thin air behind the stream of flame that shot ahead of him by at least forty feet. He'd strapped a polished metal tank, like a fire extinguisher, to his back. In his left hand he held out a long metal pipe that was connected to the tank by a thick black hose, while his right feverishly pumped a handle that stuck out from the side of the contraption. "Get behind me and keep firing!"

Even from this distance, I could feel the heat of the burning orange stream. O'Brian swept the nozzle left to right, painting the roadway. Mesmerized by the undulating orange flames, I watched as the gremlins turned in writhing panic. They attacked the oily flames that engulfed them. As soon as one emerged from the patch of incinerated pavement, it would drop lifeless to the ground, in conjunction with numerous shots that rang out from the reformed firing line.

I shook my head, pulling myself back to reality, and fired. The distinctive spit and sputter of an aircraft engine shutting down drew my attention skyward. The radio crackled with static.

"Widowmaker Actual, RAF FV992, we have an emergency."

I looked up and spotted flames and black smoke rolling from the B-25's left engine.

Chapter 14

Shortly before dark, we rendezvoused back at the Chevrolet farm with the aircrews of both aircraft. April, Carmen, and Grand-mère Monette happily appeared in the doorway and waved from the porch of the small farmhouse as we pulled up. Pierce had escorted the damaged and slow-moving B-25 Mitchell back and passed along approach instructions for landing at the farm, which we'd started to refer to affectionately as Chevy Field.

Captain Reginald Sizemore the Third, the volunteered British SAS team member who'd been sent back to us from Chippelle Airfield with the last load of supplies, had been overly ecstatic at the sight of a British aircraft flying overhead. I could have sworn I heard the man squeal with a sigh of relief. He promptly popped to attention, saluted the craft as she flew overhead on her orientation pass, then hurried back into the barn, muttering something about a fresh batch of tea. That actually sounded pretty good to me after a long and dreadfully grueling mission. The captain panicked slightly when Lieutenant Rustay called his name and waved him over. He promised he'd only be a moment to put the kettle on. The LT waved him on and began unloading his gear.

I had a fairly good idea of what the LT wanted with Captain Sizemore. See, after we'd finished mopping up the remaining gremlins that survived both bombings and O'Brian's homemade flamethrower, the LT had to calm the surviving members of Kilo Squad. What that had pushed the guys past the breaking point was when one of the still burning gremlins leapt through the wall of flames in a full-on headlong charge, landing on Lieutenant Byrd's face. The gremlin made quick work of the recon team commander, shredding the man's face with ravenous furry. It then immediately pounced from Lieutenant Byrd to the bookie private named Ronny, removing the man's throat with one swipe of its razor-sharp claws.

Rustay took pity on the remaining recon members, bringing them back to camp with us, and promised to carry them on to Chippelle Field at the first opportunity. Though each of them had been trained and prepared to face the carnage and emotional trauma of the battlefield like the rest of us, no amount of training could prepare a man to face a gremlin horde with the instinctual intention to devour anything in its path. Maybe the rest of us were certifiably insane? Maybe something else in our past had mentally prepared us to witness the unknown? Maybe it's just the amount of bad and cruel shit each of us had been exposed to. I'd been called cold-hearted and emotionally detached by a few girls I'd dated in the past.

Once, when I was young, my paw and me had been delivering goods to a farm on the far side of Lookout Mountain down near to Fort Payne, Alabama. It was a nice enough and memorable trip for the most part. I was probably around seven or eight, and the two-day trip had, up to that point, been unexciting. I'll never forget that trip, though, and not just for what happened at the end of it. The days of travel and camping out under the stars with my old man always came to mind whenever I looked up at the starlit sky. It was a good time spent with a good man. Just us.

We talked about school and how things work on different types of farms. He'd had a lot of experience over the years doing a lot of different types of work, but especially farming. Everything from growing cotton, to hay, to tobacco and corn. After we'd gotten where we were going for the delivery, the landowner had his hired men, a handful of black fellas, unload the wagon. They'd gotten the crates and sacks off, unloading them down by the barn, while the landowner took us up to the big house to sit a spell on the porch and enjoy some of his wife's delicious sweet tea.

Well, these hired hands pulled our wagon up to the bottom of the porch steps and started to untie the last piece of cargo. I hadn't seen it before, because the wagon had already been loaded by the time I'd climb on board with my paw, but when they pulled back the heavy blanket covering the thing, my jaw dropped. Beneath the blanket on that whole trip was a gorgeously ornate mahogany desk. Its top was this beautifully designed starburst inlaid with sections of red oak, poplar, maple, walnut, and black locust. My seven-year-old mind was absolutely sure it had been lacquered a dozen times and polished for days before being loaded.

Widowmakers

Four of the landowner's hired men climbed into the wagon and began moving the heavy but delicate piece of furniture. Being extra careful, they moved it inches at a time, with two of the men climbing to the ground as they inched it to the rear of the wagon. I watched the workers in amazement while my paw and the landowner continued their conversation of the latest news from Chattanooga.

The large, muscular men reluctantly lifted the heavy desk and stepped back away from the wagon. The entire process had been going well, until the smallest of the workers, who was on the ground, slipped on a patty of horse manure. The weight of the desk shifted, and the man fell backward. The corner of the desk came down on the man's chest and pinned him to the cobblestone path that lead up to the house. His screams of pain were easily overshadowed by the angry shouts of the landowner, who was immediately on his feet and sprinting down the porch steps.

When I asked my paw what was going on, he told me to just be quiet and mind myself, that this was no business of ours. We were just waiting to be paid so we could get back on the road and get back home. The landowner proceeded to scream at the young black man, calling him a clumsy idiot and saying he wished he could find better help around here. While looking over the desk for damage, the landowner found where the black man's fingernails had scratched into the side of the desk. He exploded with a roar of anger, then kicked the pinned man in the side of the head more times than I could count. I remember the side of his face looked like something my maw had run through the sausage grinder at home.

Obviously unconscious, the black man convulsed and coughed, spitting out blood as he gasped and wheezed as life came back to him. Then the landowner erupted at the splattering of blood on the side of his brand-new desk. He planted the heel of his boot square in the hired man's face, then pulled an old Navy service Colt from his pocket, and promptly shot the worker in the side of the head. With a sigh of disgust, he returned the revolver to his pocket, ordered the others to clean up the mess and get the desk moved, then he turned back to me and my paw, apologizing for the shoddy condition of his hired help.

Since then, nothing has really ever seemed to phase me. Things just were how they were, and you pressed on and did whatever needed to be done without question. That's just how it was.

Needless to say, the LT, being authorized by Colonel Archer to recruit others in the field as necessary to fulfill the mission, didn't think any of the remaining recon guys would make good team member candidates. But the bomber crew, on the other hand, hadn't cracked under pressure, even when being chased down and attacked by flying gremlins.

During the drive back to Chevy Field, Lieutenant Rustay picked my brain about the capabilities and limitations of the B-25 Mitchell bombers. He'd heard how some of our guys in the Pacific theater had some real success with modifications to the aircraft in the field. They'd done things like adding weapons points and changing out the payload, turning them into more of an attack craft than a bomber. He asked my opinion on the possible benefits of having one, and her crew, in our inventory. My answer was with a little elbow grease and ingenuity, we could have air to ground superiority against machine and monster alike. He apparently liked that answer, because he smiled wide as he watched the injured medium bomber glide in for a smooth and gentle landing.

"I apologize for that, Commander," Captain Sizemore said, appearing behind me and the LT as we watched the bomber taxi along the grass field. I yelled for Perunko to go over and marshal the bomber in like I'd explained, and he eagerly took off at a trot to the open field that made up the dooryard of the small farmhouse. I started to turn around to listen to Sizemore, but then glanced back at the sound of radial engines being throttled up. Pierce banked *Jess's* nose up and left, bringing her back around into the pattern to line up for a final landing approach. There was just something about that airplane I'd never get enough of. I don't think I could ever get tired of watching her soar through the sky. Finally pulling my head out of the clouds, I turned to face Captain Sizemore and the LT.

"It's quite alright, Captain," Lieutenant Rustay said with a wave before crossing his arms. "Your countrymen handled themselves exceptionally well during their first encounter with the supernatural. If I see someone who could be a beneficial addition to our team and could increase our mission effectiveness, I have authorization from Colonel Archer to recruit them as I see fit. The only catch is they must have already faced a supernatural threat on the battlefield. Unlike the remaining members of the recon squad we saved, the crew of the British bomber has impressed me."

"I am afraid to speculate at any length as to what my countrymen may or may not decide, Commander," Sizemore said nervously.

"I'm not a commander, Sizemore," Lieutenant Rustay grumbled.

"You're the commander of this unit, therefore you've earned the title as such, regardless of your pay grade, sir."

"Not something I care to argue about for the moment," Rustay said. "Do you have any suggestions as to the best way to approach the subject with them?"

"Upfront and direct I suppose would be the most effective method, sir," Sizemore said, placing his hand on his chest and bowing slightly. "I'm afraid I would be the absolutely wrong person to speak with regarding human nature, sir."

"Not much of a people person, Captain?" I asked.

"No, Sergeant. At least not a particularly *good* people person," Sizemore admitted. "The professor who suggested I should join the SAS upon graduation said as much. He once commented that I'd rather spend my time with stacks of papers and reports than have a pint with a chum. And he was right, I suppose." He nodded his head as his eyes drifted away momentarily in thought.

"Which is one of the reasons Colonel Archer sent you back to us," Rustay said. "You'll be able to filter through field reports and find the ones we should follow up on and investigate."

"If you'll excuse me, Commander, I should probably get back inside and whip up something for the team," Sizemore said. "I'm sure they're all famished after the mission."

I turned to the LT, then back to Sizemore. "That's not a half-bad idea there, Reggie." He scowled at the bastardizing of his name. "Could be a damn good way to soften up the bomber crew."

The LT tapped a finger to his lips as he thought. "You're right, that's a brilliant idea, Captain. Please use whatever you need from the fresh stores. I believe there was a bottle of wine and a wheel of cheese in there as well."

"Yes, sir!" Sizemore spun on his heels and hurriedly hightailed it back to the barn.

"What do you think, LT?"

"I think I can order them to join the team if need be, but I'd rather not abuse my authority," Rustay said. "Forcing a man to a cause is no way to earn his loyalty, only his contempt."

I joined Pierce and Perunko in the post-flight inspection of the aircraft and assessed the damage to the bomber's engine. The creatures had torn away a good portion of the cowling and had started chewing into the wiring. It looked like the engine itself was fine, just some minor damage to wires and oil lines. It would take a little time to do the repairs, not to mention to get the parts, but it wasn't anything I couldn't handle.

Between the efforts of Captain Sizemore and April, we had a sizeable little feast on our hands in no time. Doyle and Grabowski set up a makeshift table made from sawhorses and planks of wood, along with seats made from barrels and crates they found stored in the barn. You could almost say it was a postcard-perfect moment, and left to his passions, Private Kenneth Doyle set up his camera on a tripod to capture the moment as if it were the Last Supper of the Second Great War. Our team sat to one side of the table, with the four men of the British bomber crew at the other end. April, Carmen, and Grand-mère Monette mingled between the crews, with the remaining members of Recon Squad Kilo interspersed throughout the group, as Captain Sizemore dished out bowls of a decadent-smelling lamb stew.

We laughed like we hadn't laughed in a long while, swapping stories of the war and of our lives before the war. After we'd finished with the main meal, even Grand-mère Monette felt compelled to tell a story from the days when she was a young girl on this farm. April translated her tale, while we sipped at a forty-year-old bottle of wine and nibbled at crackers covered with the soft, pungent Livarot cheese that April had made herself. It was a pleasant distraction and removal from the war, even if only for a short time.

In the dimming light of evening, a number of side conversations continued. Hollywood, Grabowski, and

Doyle stood off to the side of the picnic area, passing a baseball Grabowski, a die-hard Cubs fan, had brought with him from home. One of the British airmen offered odds on which Yankee would drop the ball first, and they began placing their bets. Even Sizemore and O'Brian added a bet to the pot, both betting against the young private Doyle.

"Was this your first encounter with the supernatural?" Lieutenant Rustay asked Nigel Garrick, the pilot and flight commander of the Royal Air Force bomber.

"It was, actually," Garrick said in a contemplative tone. "Granted, we'd heard of the things before. Rumors, idle chatter and the like. Some thought it was simply propaganda made up by the Germans—scuttlebutt, you see. But never in my wildest dreams could I have imagined such a thing was real."

"None of us did, Captain," I added. "At least, not until the damn things were trying to eat us. I lost my entire unit to those gremlins before the LT found me. For whatever reason, I was the one that got lucky."

"I'm sorry to hear that, Sergeant," Garrick said with a nodded bow as he dug into his pocket and produced a pipe and tobacco bag. "I truly am. And the name is Nigel, if you please. I'm not such a stickler for protocol that I have a rod up my ass like some of the officers I've known." He smiled, then distractedly stuffed the pipe, packing tobacco into the polished rosewood bowl.

"What would you and your crew think about hunting those things and things like them on a regular basis?" Rustay asked.

Nigel chuckled as he sucked on the pipe, lighting the dried tobacco. White puffs of smoke escaped from the side of his mouth. "If you haven't noticed yet, there's a war on, mate."

"I'm fully aware there's a war going on, Captain," the LT said sarcastically.

"Then why would you bloody well ask me something like that?"

"Because these creatures are still out there hampering our efforts to win the war, along with many more, from what I'm told," Rustay said in a straightforward manner. "Per Colonel Archer of Task Force 13, another team came across a bridge troll they had to remove before Allied forces could continue to the city of Caen."

Nigel looked up at Lieutenant Rustay through the puffs of pipe smoke with a sideways glance. "A bloody *troll* you say?"

"A troll."

Nigel uncomfortably shifted as he quietly puffed on his pipe in thought. "I have to admit, that is both exciting and terrifying at the same time, Lieutenant."

"Craig," the LT said.

Nigel nodded.

"Even the possibility that the things of childhood nightmares are real is as frightening as Nazi rule over Europe."

"By dealing with these things on the battlefield, we keep our brothers in arms from dealing with them. And as we've already seen, not everyone can handle the truth about these things," Rustay said, motioning toward the remaining members of the recon team. "I've been authorized by Colonel Archer to recruit those that I see fit to our team. I'd like to invite you and your crew to join the Widowmakers."

"How is that possible, exactly?" Nigel asked in a perplexed tone.

"We have special permissions," the LT said with a smile. "If we want it, we generally get it with a requisition form."

"But what about the war effort? The Jerrys have bombed my country and killed my countrymen for years. What if our one bomber is the one that makes a difference?"

"You'd still be making a difference, just in a manner that doesn't lead directly to killing Germans."

"Well that's just a bloody damned shame, now isn't it?"

The soldiers cheered as Hollywood dropped the ball, and they gathered around one of the British airmen at the end of the table to collect their winnings.

"Don't forget my cut of the fags, Gus," Nigel said, stretching his hand across the makeshift table, awaiting his winnings. The British sergeant deposited six cigarettes into the captain's hand.

"Do you gamble often, Nigel?" Rustay asked with a conniving grin.

"What man doesn't when the odds are in your favor?" Nigel said, carefully placing the cigarettes into a silver case that he quickly tucked back into his shirt pocket.

"Ever played baseball, Nigel?"

Chapter 15

Being the type of man who could rarely turn down a bet, Captain Nigel Garrick accepted Lieutenant Rustay's wager for the services of his aircraft and crew on a simple game of sandlot baseball. The rules were simple. The LT, Pierce, Hollywood, Grabowski, Doyle, Perunko, and I were to stand our ground in a ten-inning game against the Brits. Captain Garrick discussed the wager with his bombardier and navigator, Flight Sergeant Ephraim Tuttle, a short, slightly husky fellow from Hessle. Though he wasn't the athletic type, he seemed intrigued by the proposition. Both Sergeant Utah Hurst—the bomber's radio operator, from Duxford—and Sergeant Augustus "Gus" Whittaker from Crosby agreed to the terms of the challenge. To even out the number of players a bit more, we loaned the Brits both Captain Sizemore and Lance-Corporal O'Brian.

Just after dawn the following morning, the combatants gathered on the battlefield. April and Carmen had gotten up early to make a special breakfast of fruit pastries for the crew, and each man eagerly wolfed them down. Before the sun had risen far above the horizon and the dew could evaporate, the game had begun. O'Brian, being the Jack-of-all-trades he'd proved himself to be on more than a few occasions, had whittled out a roughly shaped bat that bore more of a resemblance to a cricket bat than a baseball bat. But as I learned at a young age, in sandlot rules, beggars can't be choosers.

The game had finally begun. Excited cheers and yelled curses rang out, accompanying each pop fly, stolen base, and distracted jeers from the opposing team. In just over an exciting and intense hour of play, Private Kenneth Doyle hit the baseball with such force that it had to have traveled nearly the distance of a football field, breaking our one and only bat.

Reluctant and ashamed, Captain Garrick gracefully accepted the British team's defeat. With the shaking of hands, he consigned himself, his crew, and his ship to the service of Task Force 13 and the Widowmakers, as agreed upon between himself and Lieutenant Rustay. Before midmorning, the LT, Perunko, the crew of the British bomber, and the remainder of Recon Team Kilo had loaded up into the truck and left for Chippelle Field. Besides returning the recon guys to the Regular Army, the LT was going to take care of the transfer paperwork for the B-25 and her crew. I hoped he would remember to submit the requisition list of replacement parts I'd given him for the bomber before they left.

Me and Pierce stayed back at Chevy Field to figure out how to best improve the bomber to suit the needs of our unique missions. O'Brian's suggestion was to just add more guns, which I had to agree was always a good idea, but we didn't want to overload her to the point she couldn't take off, or in any way that might compromise the airframe.

We discussed what we'd heard about how the crews in the Pacific theater had modified the aircraft to become airborne gunships, sporting dozens of extra guns, including the addition of small artillery pieces. I really wanted to see what a small howitzer would do from an airborne weapons platform, but Pierce reminded me more than a few times that we only had a handful of .50 caliber M2s and two spare 20mm cannons we'd salvaged from the remains of the aircraft back at Jackson Field.

"We could always try to salvage some of the German equipment we come across in the field," Pierce suggested.

"That won't work long term," I said. "We'd be too limited on ammo and spare parts to make that a feasible option."

"Good point," Pierce said, sighing in agreement as he stretched backward. He stood up from the large table we'd salvaged from one of the nearby gremlin-destroyed towns. The LT had sent Hollywood, Doyle, and Grabowski out on salvage duty one day to acquire some of the more basic comforts of home, like a kitchen table and chairs to sit on instead of crates or bales of hay. We'd set up a small kitchen area at one end of the barn on the ground floor, with the large table in the center of the open room.

"We could always have O'Brian rig up more of those firebombs," Pierce said as he poured a cup of coffee from the percolator pot that sat on top of the old cast iron stove. "Coffee?"

"No thanks," I said, waving off the offer. "After seeing how effective those bombs were last time, I'd expect that to be a given. We just need to keep an eye out when we're on missions for anything O'Brian can use to make new ones."

I looked back over my shoulder at the sound of the latch being opened on the large barn door. April slipped through the opening and gave each of us an annoyed glance.

Pierce sat down his coffee cup and took a step in her direction. "Is everything alright?"

She stepped back awkwardly, holding her hand up for Pierce to stop. "Could I have a word with you for just a moment?"

"Absolutely…" Pierce leapt forward, but stopped the instant her fiery glare struck him.

"Not you," she said, pointing at Pierce. "If you have a moment, Sergeant, I'd like to speak to you," she said to me directly, "in private please." Her eyes locked onto Pierce as she opened the barn door and slipped back outside.

I glanced up at Pierce, who stood there, a look of confused concern contorting his face. "What the hell did you do?"

"I have no earthly idea," he said, then sat back down at the table.

I slapped the tabletop and stood. "Guess I should go find out, then." April stood out in the dooryard, staring off blankly at the aircraft. She turned back in my direction at the sound of the barn door closing. A worried smile crossed her face, like one of those fake worried smiles wives show the public when their husbands are shipped off to war.

I slipped my hands into my pockets and slowly walked over in her direction. "Is everything alright, April?"

She craned her neck to look around me, intently watching the barn door as I approached like she was worried I'd been followed. Nervously she wrung her hands, then finally tucked them into her apron. "Not here," she said, then turned and walked toward the house.

Concerned, I watched her walk away for a moment before following behind. She opened the front door and motioned for me to continue inside.

"Please, we can talk inside." She looked past me in the direction of the barn, then glanced back up at me with pleading blue eyes.

"Has Pierce done something?" A wave of worried anger began building in my guts. My mind raced with the worst possible reasons for her odd behavior, and my insides began to painfully knot and twist. Unconsciously I started to roll up my sleeves, preparing for a fight.

She started at my reaction and quickly closed the door. "Oh no, nothing of the sort, Sergeant. I…" Her words trailed off in thought. She took a seat at the table in the kitchen of the small farmhouse. Calming herself, she looked up at me with a deadly serious stare.

"I would like to make something special for James for his birthday," she said. "I overheard him speaking of spending his birthday in a war zone to one of the other soldiers who was here."

"Okay? James who?" I looked at her with what I'm sure was a confused look of discombobulation and was otherwise wordless at her revelation.

"James. JJ?" she said questioningly. "Warrant Officer Pierce." She angrily glared at me.

"Oh, okay. Pierce. Now we're on the same page."

Her mouth twitched with what I guessed was annoyance. "You seem to be the closest to him out of all of you. Do you know what his favorite meal might be?"

I blinked at her as the information absorbed into my confused mind, then it hit me like a brick. I sucked in a long breath of revelation. "I have no idea what his favorite would be, though I can without a doubt say that any of us would appreciate a hot home-cooked meal. And I can honestly say, no matter what you make, I'm sure he'll love it. Any of us would."

She smiled. Her shoulders relaxed, and she let out a long sigh of relief.

"Oh, that's wonderful news," she said, patting her chest. "I've been so unsure of what to do that it's nearly made me sick with worry. You're all here, freeing my country from the Nazis. There's no reason we shouldn't celebrate his birthday, or any of yours, for that matter," she said, quickly catching herself.

April's little sister Carmen skipped into the small kitchen from another room at the back of the house. She swaddled and rocked a bundle in the crook of her arm as if it were an infant. Even amid the stresses of war and the insanity of our encounters with the gremlins, the young girl smiled, giggled, and enjoyed her childhood. She said something in French to April, who promptly melted with the prideful look of a parent. April turned in her seat and opened a trap door in the floor, fetching a covered metal milk pitcher from the cool cellar below the floor. Removing the lid, she poured a small amount into a tin cup that sat abandoned on the table and placed it near Carmen.

"Merci beaucoup," Carmen said happily with a quick curtsy. She scooched a chair out from the table and sat with us. Softly she began to hum a lullaby tune as she loosened the swaddle at the end near the crook of her arm, exposing a tuft of fluffy white fur hidden beneath the dull gray cloth. April watched her younger sister with prideful admiration as she dipped her finger into the cup of milk, then placed it inside the swaddle as if offering the sweet liquid to a babe.

"Did one of the barn cats have a litter of kittens?" I asked, stretching my neck for a better view.

April shrugged at my question, shaking her head with a confused look. "We don't have any cats."

We both looked back to the young girl, who giggled as she continued to hum and offer a dampened finger to the bundle. We could both hear the sound of something lazily suckling.

"Qu'est-ce que tu as là, Carmen?" April asked.

Carmen looked up at us. "Un bébé lapin," she said with a smile, then continued humming. I looked back to April.

"She said it's a baby bunny."

A chill rolled up my spine at a sudden thought. I leaned over the table, trying to get a better look. "Can we see the bunny?" I asked Carmen as calmly as I could muster.

April quickly translated for me. Carmen nodded and carefully pulled back the folds of cloth. Snuggled deep inside the heavy gray fabric, all I could see from my angle was a fluffy white ball of fur that rose and fell as the thing breathed in its warm, swaddled slumber. Carmen gently stroked the top of the fuzzy head as she coaxed the thing awake. She mumbled something in French under her breath to it, nuzzling her nose against the fuzzy head. The bundle began to squirm and stretch. A long, muscular rear leg extended from the bundle, then it reared back its head in a wide, stretching yawn. Row upon row of translucent, needle-like teeth gleamed in the dim light of the farmhouse.

April trembled and sucked in a terrified breath. Her fingernails dug into the top of the wooden table. Primordial fear overwhelmed her as a shriek born from the depths of her soul escaped.

The snow-white gremlin kit recoiled from the sound, hissed, then bounded from Carmen's arms. It bounced off the table and out of the partially open kitchen window.

Chapter 16

"**P**ierce! O'Brian!" I shouted as I raced out of the small farmhouse toward the barn. I glanced around for what must be a white speck in the distance by this point. The thing was fast, faster than any cat or jackrabbit I'd ever seen before. I didn't see it near the planes, or anywhere around the front of the farmhouse. Then I spotted it. A fast-moving puff of white heading north across the fields we'd been using as a landing strip. "Hey!" The barn doors bowed inward from the impact as I reached them, sliding to a stop against the worn wood. I fumbled with the latch and darted inside, heading straight for where I'd left my gear hanging on a nail near our makeshift kitchen area. "Grab your gear!"

Pierce stared at me like I'd gone mad. He quickly gathered together a stack of letters that looked like he'd started and stopped again multiple times. He nervously hid them away in his pack. I stopped and looked at him questioningly, then remembered why I'd run in here. "Get your gun. We've got gremlins."

"What the hell? Here?"

"What the bloody hell is going on down there?" O'Brian shouted down through the hayloft opening in the ceiling. "I'm trying to take a nap."

Widowmakers

"Get your flamethrower!" I ordered, shouting up at the Irishman. "We may have a gremlin problem. I'll explain on the way." I strapped on my web belt with ammo pouches, slung my gear over my shoulders, and raced out the back door of the barn. Pulling the bolt back on my rifle, I made sure it was loaded, then let the bolt slide back into place. I sprinted for the last place I saw the running snowball. The ground was entirely too hard to show prints, but after a brief search, I found where the grass had been bent, broken, and otherwise disturbed. I looked back toward the house and barn, then turned and looked in the direction the creature had taken, which led into the surrounding forest. I'd just crossed into the tree line when O'Brian and Pierce caught up, both of them gasping for breath after their sprint across the field.

"Would you please be explaining to me why in the bloody hell we're running after the wee little buggers?"

"What he said," Pierce gasped, rubbing at a stitch in his side.

"Because I think what I saw was a kit. At least that's my guess, since I haven't seen one with fluffy, snow-white fur before."

"A kit," Pierce said questioningly with a shake of his head.

"A kit," I said, pressing forward into the forest.

"A wee babe," O'Brian explained.

"Exactly," I continued, "just like a rabbit. Which is what they more or less look like."

I stopped, examining the ground at my feet.

"What's wrong?" Pierce asked.

"I've lost the trail."

O'Brian moved up next to me and examined the forest floor ahead of us. "There," he said, pointing off to my right. "See where the leaves have been turned over?"

I followed the direction he'd pointed and spotted the sign he'd so obviously seen. "How about you go ahead and lead this monkey show. You're a better tracker than I am. I didn't even see this until I was on top of it."

"Will do, Sergeant," the Irishman said, taking the lead in our search.

We continued for what I guess was just over a half-mile, when we came across an area where the forest floor looked like a herd of stampeding cattle had crashed through it. Small bushes and undergrowth had been shredded or trampled, leaves throughout the area were disturbed, and the bark of some of the surrounding trees had been clawed and chewed away in places.

"I think we found where it was going," Pierce whispered.

"Yup," I said, just as quietly.

"There," O'Brian said, pointing toward a grouping of large stones that stood out from the rolling hillside. "I can smell them from here." Slinging his rifle, O'Brian reached over his shoulder and grabbed the nozzle of the flamethrower. With a quick flick of his flip lighter along his pant leg, he lit the pilot flame.

I sniffed and could barely make out a musky scent mingled with decay that hung in the still summer air. I double-checked my rifle and my revolver, then dropped my pack, retrieving my flashlight and two grenades, which I hung on my belt. Pierce followed my lead and did the same.

"You fellas ready?" I asked, then turned to each of them.

Pierce sighed, cracked his neck, and held his rifle at the ready. "As ready as I'm going to get, I suppose."

"Aye," the Irishman said, then took a swig from his flask and tucked it away again. An eager grin crossed his face. "Let's get to it so I can get back to my nap before the day is over."

Pierce snorted a laugh, then without another word, I marched forward toward the stones. We gave the outcropping a wide berth, keeping our distance as we circled around, investigating the area. Tattered remains of uniforms lay scattered about the forest floor. American, British, Canadian, and German, all stained dark from the dried blood soaked into their fibers. Moving a few feet to my left, I could plainly see the opening to a cave mouth at the base of the small rise.

"Sure looks like another nest to me," I said, then flicked on my flashlight and moved quickly to the side. Bits of bones littered the area just in front of the opening. It was going to be a tight squeeze at first, but looked like it opened up a few feet in. I looked down at the rifle in my hand and contemplated leaving it at the cave mouth.

"What's wrong?" Pierce asked.

I looked back into the depths of the cave and shifted my position to get a different view. "I'm not sure we'll have room in there for rifles."

"If we don't have room for rifles, O'Brian doesn't have room for that deathtrap he's carrying," Pierce whispered with a quiet laugh.

"Fair point," I said.

"I'll not step a bloody foot in there without my dear Shelly." O'Brian lovingly caressed the nozzle of the homemade flamethrower.

We both looked back at the Irishman with what I'm sure was a concerned look of confusion. I shrugged, then turned my attention back to the hole.

"Might as well." I sighed. "It might get to the point that every shot counts in there. Especially after O'Brian lights them up with his flamethrower."

Pierce nudged me forward. "Let's just get this over with. If we get into a bind, we can always dump them inside."

I nodded and crouched, waddling my way into the opening. The musky stench of the creatures was much worse inside the cave. I slid down a small incline that opened up into a larger chamber about six feet down. The cave had to be at least ten degrees cooler than the summer air outside. The layers of limestone glistened with moisture that clung to nearly every surface. The chamber continued through a narrow path to the right of the opening that angled downward. Cloth from uniforms, bits of leather, bone fragments, and more littered the slick cave floor. I turned back to Pierce and O'Brian. They both answered my questioning look with a nod. So I continued slowly into the opening. My foot slid on the snot-slick surface of the cave floor, and I went spiraling down the slope. Turning so I was feet first on my rear as I slid downward, I nearly dropped my flashlight. The steep path turned to the left and opened out, followed by a sudden drop-off into a deep, dark abyss. My hands reflexively shot out, pressing hard against the sides of the crevice to slow my descent. My palms burned from the sudden scouring over the limestone walls. I backpedaled, my feet slipping on the slimy stone of the path. Securing myself against the side of the opening, I held up my light and panned it around the room. Flowing water had done its job over thousands of years to carve out the breathtaking cathedral I found myself in. Hundreds, even thousands of beautiful stalactites glistened as I shined the light about. Carefully I leaned forward and looked over the edge of the stony outcropping. Just twenty or so feet below me, a subterranean stream flowed at a fairly good pace. To the left of where I perched, a series of ledges stuck out from the side of the cavern, where it had broken off at some point in the distant past, leaving a perfect if slightly jagged climbing surface.

"Sullivan," O'Brian said from above. I looked back up the chute just in time to see a rope plummet down the path toward me. Grabbing the rope, I slid it over the edge toward the water below. The line went taut and I tugged on it to check the security.

"Got it," I said in a shouted whisper. "Come down slow. The whole joint is slimy and wet down here."

"Coming down," Pierce said as he clumsily stumbled down the chute, and I was able to snag his arm and stop his descent.

"How the hell are you a pilot with two left feet?"

He shrugged at me. "Flying is just something that comes naturally to me."

"Hold up, O'Brian," I said back up the hole, then leaned, glancing over the edge to see where the end of the rope had landed. A good foot or so of it flipped about in the rushing water. I pulled myself upright and looked to Pierce.

"Think you can make it down there?"

He wrapped the rope around his wrist and peered over the edge. "Are you sure we *want* to go down there? How hard is it going to be to get back up, or what if we get trapped down there?"

"You aren't turning yellow on me, are you?"

Pierce shot me a scornful look, then let out a reluctant breath. "No, I'm not turning yellow." He turned and began backing down the ledge and over the side of the cliff. "Hold that light so I can see what I'm doing."

I did as he'd asked, holding my flashlight in the best position I could to provide light and not shine it in the Marine's eyes. Once he'd reached the bottom, I tossed the light down to him and whispered loudly back up the hole for O'Brian to come down slowly. It wouldn't do any of us any good if that tank were to rupture and ignite while in the chute. I could just imagine it turning into a waterfall of fire flowing into the stream below and creating a billowing cloud of steam.

O'Brian shimmied his way down the chute slowly, shuffling his feet as he went.

Pierce shushed us from below. "Are you trying to let all the gremlins know we're here? Every sound you guys make is echoing down here."

I held out a thumbs up where Pierce could see, then moved to the side. O'Brian eased himself down and balance the weight of the napalm-filled tank.

In no time flat, we were both at the bottom of the chamber, standing in the frigid underground stream. To the right of where we'd entered, water bubbled and roiled up from under the rock face itself. To the left, the chamber continued into the depths of the underground. The space rose up what looked to be forty feet in the air, tapering to a point at the top, like a gash in the face of the stone wall. We pressed forward, following the flow of water through the fissure as it curved to the right, then left, and opened up into another chamber. The small stream fell away along a small drop into a dark pool that had to be all of twenty feet across. Our lights reflected oddly off the surface of the underground pond, casting eerie shadows around the chamber.

A sickly wet sucking sound drew my attention to the left of where we'd entered. There were strange, yellowish growths shaped something like a muskmelon, but their surface looked leathery and squished at the bottom, like a ball of clay dropped onto a spinning wheel. The things covered the gray limestone wall like some kind of mushroom infestation. A handful of the things visibly moved and shifted as if something was inside them.

"Blessed Mother Mary protect and deliver us," O'Brian said under his breath as he crossed himself. "What are those?"

"Egg sacks or cocoons, maybe," I said, unsure of anything at this point.

"Have you seen anything like that before?" Pierce asked, stepping over to the covered wall. He knelt and leaned in to examine the thing more closely.

"No, never. And there's hundreds of them," I said as I swept my light around the chamber.

"More like bloody thousands," O'Brian growled. He aimed his light into the deepest part of the chamber. "Sullivan, what do you make of that?"

Me and Pierce both turned our lights to point where O'Brian had stopped. The small Irishman squinted in the dim light, attempting to focus on something at the other side of the chamber.

"I'll be damned," Pierce whispered. "Is the wall on that side *moving*?"

The sound of something being torn like ripping cloth reverberated throughout the chamber from directly behind us. A gurgled bark seemingly answered from somewhere deep within the cavern, followed by other chitters and barks. I turned back to the wall of melon-shaped growths. They were still there, still intact, except for one. Movement drew my attention to the chamber entrance. At about chest high, I watched as a ragged slit continued to open longways across the top of the thing's round surface. It shifted and flexed like a snake in an egg as it moved and rolled inside the thing. Viscous yellow mucus seeped slowly from the still expanding gash. It shook, then split open the rest of the way, revealing a tiny pink nose that sniffed at the damp subterranean air.

Pierce raised his rifle and aimed, but I placed my hand on top of the barrel and pushed it back down.

"What the hell, Sullivan? It needs to die."

"Bloody hell right it needs to die," O'Brian said, then spat at the wall. "Let me burn the whole bloody lot of the wee devils."

"Hold on." I motioned for the other two to wait. "Maybe we can learn a thing or two about these things before we destroy them." I slung my rifle and took a step closer, holding the light to get a better look through the opening in the melon-shaped cocoon. The tip of the thing blossomed open all of a sudden, and a soggy mass of tangled white fur slid from the opening. I placed my hands beneath the cocoon just as the furry white mass slithered out and landed in my cupped palms. The thick, sticky fluid oozed through my fingers.

Ya know, it's strange how something will spur an old memory and bring it to the front of your mind out of nowhere. I started to think back on all the animals I'd helped to birth over the years, from calves, to colts, to standing watch over a new clutch of chicks as they broke out of their tiny prisons. But at that moment, I thought back to the first time I ever helped to birth anything. When I was still little, we'd taken in this tiny stray kitten that looked like it was half-starved when I found it hiding under our porch. My paw wasn't too happy when he saw me carrying her around. He especially wasn't happy when he realized I'd already named her Snow, for her snowy white fur. She cried for days and would only be quiet when I held her, or if she'd fallen asleep on my chest, suckling the collar of my shirt. Paw said that was a sure sign she'd been separated from her mother too early.

The following year she'd apparently had herself a midnight rendezvous with a tomcat, or hell, my paw swore the tom had to be a bobcat, as big as her belly was. She was a tiny cat compared to some I'd seen around the area, and her belly was so round it dragged on the ground as she walked. When the time had come, she'd found her spot to have the kittens, and I set myself up right next to her. Whispering, I promised her I'd be there the entire time.

Somewhere in the dark hours of the morning, she went into labor, and the first kitten began its journey into the world. Snow meowed at me as I caught the first kitten, dried it, and began to rub its back like my paw had taught me. It felt like I must have stared straight at that first slimy ball of fur for hours. I rubbed its back and whispered encouraging words to the stiff little newborn.

It's funny. I hadn't even thought about that moment in years.

Paw helped Snow finish birthing the rest of her first litter, while I rubbed the back of the stillborn kitten. I must have kept at the gentle strokes for over an hour, but the kitten never did take its first breath. Neither did any of the others in that first litter. Paw gently took the kitten from me and placed it in an old shoebox with its twelve siblings. We had a small service for the kittens out back of the house in the morning, after we'd caught a few hours of shuteye, then buried them in the family graveyard right next to my maw. She'd always loved cats, and we both figured she could use the company up there, and they'd need someone to snuggle up with and give them scratches.

Memories are a real funny kinda thing, ya know.

I let out a halfhearted laugh and wiped away a tear when I realized the kit was breathing. My thumb had been reflexively stroking the fuzzy white back of the baby gremlin the whole time. It stretched its legs out and rolled its head to the left, then flopped to the right.

"Hey there, little guy," I whispered to the kit and continued to gently stroke its back. I held it up level with my eyes so I could examine it more closely. As far as I could tell, short of the color of the creature's fur, it looked identical to the adults we'd seen, even down to the rows of needle-like teeth it displayed with its first yawn.

It let out a sudden, shrieking wail so loud it felt like my ears were going to bleed. I dropped the kit to the cave floor and immediately stomped the noise out of the thing.

Barks, chirps, and other shrill cries answered the call of the newborn gremlin.

"Um, Sullivan," Pierce said as he put his back against the wall.

I grabbed Pierce by the sleeve and pulled him out of the chamber. "Light 'em up, O'Brian."

"Gladly, Lad."

I could feel the heat of the flames as the orange glow grew brighter in the other chamber. The stream of burning liquid shot out from the tip of the homemade flamethrower through the open portal. The wall at the opposite side of the pond writhed with the shadows of rushing forms.

"We gotta go!" I yanked on Pierce's sleeve, then sprinted as fast as I could back up into the large cathedral chamber. Taking a stance in the cold stream, I waited, my rifle at the ready as best as I could with my flashlight in my left hand.

"Get up the rope, I've got you covered," I ordered as Pierce entered the chamber. He stepped back with a start at first, noticing the rifle pointed in his general direction.

Eagerly the young warrant officer climbed the rope and secured himself on the ledge.

"Come on, Sullivan!"

Orange flashes glowed brightly down the corridor. I looked up at Pierce.

"Go, get out of here! We'll be right behind you!"

Pierce puffed out a reluctant breath, then started to climb. "You just make sure you're both right behind me!" he shouted, disappearing into the upper chamber.

And if worse came to worst, he could still tell the others what had happened to me and O'Brian.

The Irishman suddenly appeared at the far end of the tunnel, then fired another burst of liquid flames toward the pond. He turned and ran in my direction.

"The bloody little buggers are right behind me." He panted as he splashed to a stop.

"Do you have anything left in that tank?"

"Aye, another good shot or two, I'd guess." Still gasping for breath, he rapidly pumped the charging handle of the flamethrower.

The roar of the stampeding gremlins as they charged through the cavern was almost deafening. I could see the creatures rushing up the slope like they were one massive wave of bodies.

"Give 'em hell!" I fired into the mass as the entire chamber flashed a fiery orange. The side of my face ached from the heat that I'm sure had already left one hell of a burn. O'Brian held the trigger as he continued to pump the handle, flooding the tunnel full of liquid hellfire. I shoved a new clip into the chamber and slid the breech home.

The stream of the flamethrower shrank to a slow trickle by the time I emptied my next clip. "Go, I got this!" I shouted to O'Brian over the roar of flames and shrieks. The small Irishman dropped the tank and shimmied up the rope in almost nothing flat. I quickly pulled the two grenades I'd brought with us, dropped the pins, and chucked them into the heart of the fire. I don't know how, but it sure as hell felt like I floated up the rope and into the upper chamber at what must have been close to the speed of sound. Pierce and O'Brian pulled me free of the hole just as we felt the concussion of the first grenade, followed closely behind by the second explosion as it resonated through the stone.

The floor beneath our feet shook and shifted in accompaniment to a cacophonous roar that bellowed up from the depths below. Massive cracks suddenly formed in the wall and floor right in front of us. We charged headlong, stumbling as the floor crumbled beneath our feet. I leapt the final few feet out of the cave mouth, pushing O'Brian clear just as one of the large stones that made up the entrance collapsed, sealing the entrance. The entirety of the stone outcropping, along with a large portion of the hillside, then collapsed in on itself.

I dropped to my knees in the leaf litter of the forest floor and kissed the ground beneath me. "Remind me the next time I feel like crawling down in a hole how bad an idea it is to chase these things underground."

O'Brian pulled his flask from his pocket, took a long pull, and handed it to me. I took a pull of the finely-aged whiskey and passed the flask to Pierce, who took a sip and collapsed onto his back.

"Oh, hey, that's a pretty sunset," he said, looking up at the flame-red sky.

I looked around and found the sun near the horizon. "Wow, I didn't realize we'd been down there for that…," I said before being shushed by Pierce. "What?" He shushed me again. The expression that contorted his face had to be confused thought, his eyes darting back and forth as if searching through his internal database of information.

"We've got bombers inbound," Pierce said as he sat up and took another drink from the flask.

"Bombers? What are you talking about, you bloody loon? I don't hear a thing," O'Brian said, snatching his flask back from Pierce.

"Yeah, I don't hear anything either," I said, then stood.

"Please let them be ours. Please let them be ours." He stood and looked for the sun to get his bearings, then turned in the direction of the noise. "Yes! The sound is coming from the north. They have to be ours!" Pierce strolled along, shuffling his feet in the thick layer of leaves with his gaze craned skyward. "There! There they are!" he shouted, pointing in the direction of dozens of dark silhouettes flying in formation high in the sky.

"I'll be damned if that doesn't look like every B-17 bomber in the inventory," I said to no one in particular.

Oddly comforted by the sight of massive American firepower, we watched as a multitude of the colossal bombers roared overhead, heading for what we guessed was the area surrounding Paris. There had been chatter about an operation to push deep into enemy territory in order to liberate the country's capital city.

"Should we pack it up and get back to the farm?" I asked, then turned to head back the way we'd came.

"Thought you'd never ask," O'Brian said. "I have a nap to finish before the day is over."

Tired, sore, and mentally distant, we turned to start for home, when our brief relief and reverie was shattered by a discordant roar that raced across the countryside. We turned in the direction of the noise. High above the treetops, a dark shape, maybe the size of a small fighter, flapped its wings, soaring higher with every stroke in the direction of the bomber formations.

Chapter 17

I honestly don't think I've ever run that fast in my entire life. Once we saw that the large flying gremlin had what looked like a squadron of smaller flying gremlins trailing behind it, we ran like our tails were on fire and our asses were catching, then double-timed it back to the farm. Pierce and O'Brian climbed into *Jumpin' Jess* just as soon as we got back and fired her up. I sidetracked and ran to the house to let April know what was going on before climbing into the RO position on board *Jess*. In moments we roared skyward, and Pierce banked hard to the southeast in the direction of Paris.

"So what's the plan, Sullivan?" Pierce asked over the headset.

I laughed and let out a sarcastic sigh. "Are you kidding me? Have we had anything that resembled a plan up to this point?"

"Not bloody likely," O'Brian chimed in.

"No, I don't believe we have," Pierce said with a questioning tone.

"Exactly, we haven't," I continued. "We've flown by the seat of our pants so far, so why change it now?"

"Good point, I suppose," Pierce said.

"Just get us within range so we can get eyes on these things, and then we can go from there."

"Will do, Sarge," Pierce said.

We cruised at nearly full military power for about ten minutes before catching up to the gremlins and the bombers. These things were fast, and they flew in formation, like a flight of Canadian geese.

"Do you think the bomber crews see the creatures?" O'Brian asked.

"I know the standard operating procedure is to maintain radio silence until met with enemy resistance," Pierce said. "I think this might technically count as enemy resistance."

"You're probably right," I said, then flipped the switch to transmit on all frequencies. "Allied bomb group, this is Widowmaker One. We're coming up on your six, along with a flight of..." I let go of the mic switch then flipped back to the internal comms. "What the hell should I tell them?"

"Widowmaker One, this is Red Able. Please repeat, we lost you. You said a flight of what?"

"Just tell them the truth," Pierce said. "That bird in the back is about to have them crawling up their tailpipe."

"True," I said then flipped back to the main frequency. "Red Able, this is Widowmaker One. We are coming up on your six in pursuit of a flight of winged gremlins. Get your gunners on alert. You do not want these things on your wings."

"Did I just hear you correctly, Widowmaker One? Did you just say *gremlins*?"

"Yes, I did, Red Able. You have a flight of seven gremlins flying wedge formation at five o'clock low to your rear ship."

"Red Able, um… hey, Jonesy, Widowmaker One isn't shitting you, man," a new voice said with a thick Brooklyn accent. "We've got a flight of seven *somethings* crawling up our ass back here. None of the boys on our bird have ever seen anything like them before. They almost look like overgrown jackrabbits with wings. These things look wicked mean, man. Permission to open fire."

"If you know what's good for you, you'll give the order, Red Able," I said then flipped to the internal comms. "Pierce, see if you can get us ahead of those things and clear of any fire from the bombers. Stay low so I can use the turret from back here."

"Copy that, Sarge," Pierce said. The engines roared as he pushed them to max power.

"You sure I can't squeeze off a few rounds at the buggers?" O'Brian asked. "I've got them in my sights."

"If you have a clean shot, take it. Just be careful not to hit the bombers." I could hear the drive motor on the other side of the bulkhead whir to life as O'Brian took aim. Its motors hummed from the minute adjustments.

"Bollacks!" O'Brian shouted. "We'll be right under the little blighters before I can get a clean shot."

"Alright then," I said, spinning my seat to take control of the turret. "Switching control." The drive motors of the turret hummed once again, re-centering the gun on the aim of my targeting reticle.

"Get ready," Pierce shouted. "We're about to pass under them."

I turned my sights as high as I could and waited for the first of the creatures to appear in view. We unexpectedly fell sideways from the sky and slipped back to the right.

"What the hell is going on up there, Pierce?"

"Just shut up and hang on!" Pierce shouted. "The things dove at us as we passed under them."

"We've picked up a wee hitchhiker," O'Brian shouted over the comms. "Left wing, outboard of the engine."

I leaned back from the sights and looked out over the wing through the plexiglass window. The gremlin easily dug its razor-sharp claws into the aluminum surface of the wing and was making its way over the engine boom, heading in my direction.

"Hang on," Pierce shouted. "I'm gonna see if I can shake it off."

My stomach lurched as *Jumpin' Jess* rolled, inverted, and suddenly dropped from the sky. I started to think I might break the handles off the turret control as I held on for dear life. We fell, then banked sharply back to the right, then nosed skyward once again. I leaned back and looked out over the left wing.

"I think it worked, Pierce," I said. "I don't see it."

"I think you're right, lad," O'Brian added. "I don't see any sign of the bugger from up here, either."

"Alright, let's get back up to the bombers."

The sound of automatic gunfire caught my attention. I looked out the upper window of the radar operator's compartment. We'd flown far enough away from the bombers and gremlins that the gunners aboard the bombers had a clear shot at the creatures. The gremlins bobbed and weaved as they climbed higher and gained on the cruising bombers. Flashes of fire erupted from the lower ball turrets and waist gunner positions of the two nearest bombers. A sudden black cloud of mist erupted around two of the creatures. They jerked as the .50 caliber rounds of the Browning machine guns easily penetrating their fleshy bodies. As if in one last desperate attempt to protect themselves, they curled their wings around themselves and fell away to the darkening ground below.

Pierce banked us gently to the left to get into firing position. I turned the quad turret high and to the left, tracking ahead of the creatures and waiting for a clear shot. I watched as the largest of the flying gremlins gripped the underside of one of the bombers and climbed around to the side of the tail gunner's window.

I pressed the transmit button. "Bomber group," I said then looked back out at the tail of the bomber for the flight color and call letter. "Blue Charlie, you have a tick on your backside. I repeat. Blue Charlie, the mother gremlin is climbing up your ass!"

The radios were silent as I watched the creature rip away the tail gunner's canopy and climb inside the rear of the bomber.

"May God have mercy on that poor bastard's soul," O'Brian muttered over the comms. I could picture him crossing himself as I listened to his whispered prayer.

Widowmakers

As we slipped into position, we watched with horrified fascination. We could see through the waist gun opening as the mother gremlin leapt upon and shredded both of the bomber's waist gunners. She disappeared from view into the forward fuselage. It couldn't have been more than a few heartbeats before she reached the cockpit. The bomber awkwardly pitched up and rolled, yawing over onto her sister ship to her right, then the two dominoed into a third right behind that.

We rolled hard to the right. Pierce banked us so hard that we pulled what felt like over a dozen Gs as he maneuvered us out of the way of the burning wreckage of the bombers that now fell out of the sky.

"Just hold on back there," Pierce said, grunting through the maneuver.

"Not like we have a bloody choice," O'Brian growled.

The plane rolled left, leveling out for a moment, then banked gently left. I turned the seat to face aft and helplessly watched as the three heavy bombers plummeted earthward. I waited, hoping to see a chute or two billow out and catch the air as the crew escaped, but none ever did.

"Can either of you get a bead on the rest of those things?" Pierce said over the comms.

I took a deep breath and replied, "Yeah, let me see what I've got." I wiped a hand over my face, then turned back to the turret controls, and froze. Sitting there perched at the edge of the upper bulkhead on the other side of the plexiglass screen was a snarling, blood-covered gremlin that had to be every bit of twice my size.

I tried to say something into the comms to warn the other two, but my voice cracked into a dry raspy nothing. It sank its claws into *Jess* and tore away the plastic window like it was nothing more than wet newspaper. It shoved its head into the opening and let out a bestial cry unlike anything I'd ever heard before in my life. Reflexively I swung, my fist connecting with the side of the creature's face in one hell of a right hook. It hurt like hell. The thing's head whipped back and smacked the frame of the rear canopy, and it shook its head like I'd actually hit it hard enough to addle its wits.

"It's on our back!" I shouted, then unstrapped and slid out of the chair to the floor of the compartment.

"What? Where?" Pierce shouted back over the comms, and the plane suddenly nosed over into a dive, gaining speed as we raced earthward. I grabbed hold of the seat base just as we rolled hard to the right, pulled a sharp nose up, then nosed over and rolled back to the right like an alligator in a death roll. I braced myself against the side of the compartment in an attempt to keep from being beaten to death. My headset flew off as *Jess* jerked to stop the roll and pulled up once more.

"Level out!" I shouted, hanging onto the pedestal for dear life. I glanced up to see the creature squeezing into the compartment through the opening. "It's in here with me!" I shouted, hoping Pierce and O'Brian could at least hear me over the noise of the wind rushing in. It slid into the opening and dropped onto the seat. I backpedaled, pushing myself away from the creature into the bubble dome at the rear of the compartment. It let out a roaring shriek that sounded like what I imagined the damned souls of hell would sound like if they all screamed out at the same time. It leapt over me and landed against the back of the bubble dome. The unmistakable sound of cracking plastic found my battered eardrums as I turned and started to scootch back toward the seat, when the thing leapt back to the chair. Then I spotted a second one perched on the back of the aircraft where the first one had sat and examined me.

"We have another one on our back!" I shouted, hoping one of them might hear me. My hope was answered by a sharp climb that threw me back into the bubble dome. The area around two of the bolts in the lower-left corner of the dome shattered and fell away in the slipstream. I glanced back up at the bark of the gremlin mother. She hissed a growl as she dropped to the deck from the seat and stepped toward me. Three more of the bolts on the left side broke free from the cracking plastic of the dome, causing it to shake violently. The gremlin mother hissed again.

I hissed back and yelled at her with everything in me. "If I only had a gun, I'd blow your damned head off!" *Wait*... I thought, then reached down to my side and instinctively slipped the Colt Army revolver from its holster. In one swift action, I cocked the hammer, aimed, and fired a round right between the bitch's eyes as she leapt atop me and went limp.

Suddenly overloaded by what must have been equal to my own body weight as it slammed into me, the base of the aft bubble dome shattered, breaking free from its restraints.

I grabbed ahold of the rear radar mount bracket and pulled myself back into the compartment in the split second before the rushing wind caught the dome and slammed it into the leading edge of the main stabilizer. A section of skin on the top of the stabilizer ripped away and disappeared into the wind stream behind us. The mother gremlin flopped limply in the windstream, impaled on a broken wing spar that stuck up from the damaged stabilizer. I clung to the edge of the aftmost bulkhead as if my life depended on it, because it did. I hung on for dear life until I managed to step far enough into the compartment to grip the seat. I pulled myself into the seat and strapped back in. Reaching down for the headset cord, I pulled the headset back up to me and put it back on, then reactivated the turret control.

"We have some damage back here, Pierce. Missing the rear dome, and we took a hit to the stabilizer."

"I swear you must be part cockroach, Sullivan," Pierce cheerfully said. "You just won't die, will you?"

"Not if I can help it, that's for sure," I said, then aimed the turret toward the remaining airborne gremlins. "Get me lined up, Pierce. Let's finish this and go home."

"Copy that!"

Epilogue

It didn't take us long to mop up the few gremlins the bomber crews hadn't picked off while we were busy with the queen. We wished the bomber crews the best of luck, then set course back to Chevy Field. The LT and the rest of the crew had arrived while we were gone and were waiting impatiently with April for our return.

Once we pulled in and the props stopped spinning, April ran up and eagerly waited for Pierce to climb down from the cockpit. Before he hit the ground, she pounced on him like a panther stalking its prey. She pulled him in close and kissed him deeply. I politely looked away but could still hear her whispering sweet words to him in French. O'Brian began to spin a yarn for April's little sister after he dropped to the ground. He'd seen how scared and unsure she looked and decided to try to put the girl at ease. The entire crew hung on O'Brian's every word as he retold the story of how I'd almost died at the hands of the evil gremlin queen, not once, but at least three separate times. This was all made up fluff to help his version of the story along, but still, they soaked it all in. The small Irishman even growled and hissed at Carmen a few times to get a squeal out of the young girl.

As I started the walk-around inspection, Private Doyle ran up with his camera in hand, eager to document our successful mission. We removed the queen from the rear stabilizer where she'd ridden the entire return trip, and laid her out on the ground in front of the assembled group. We all stood proudly next to *Jumpin' Jess,* displaying our kill. Grabowski and Hollywood stretched her wings outward, while I held her up upright like a trophy turkey. He snapped a few pictures using the wind-up timer built into the thing, so he could be in the pictures with the rest of us.

Lieutenant Rustay came up to me as everyone scattered after the picture.

"You doing alright, Sergeant?"

"I'd have to say fair to middlin', at least," I replied.

"Then how long do you think it would take you to get her ready and airworthy?"

"Hell, LT. She could fly now, but I'd rather patch up that tail at least. Why, what's up?"

"There've been reports of extremely large birds that have attacked platoons and flown away with a soldier or two already. The colonel wants us to investigate these reports, and if possible, eliminate the problem."

"If they're anything like the gremlins, I'll gladly help."

The End

Joint Task Force 13 is a project of Three Ravens Publishing. We expect to follow this book up with a half dozen more in 2021, all written by experienced authors in many different timeframes.

Find the Origins anthology on Amazon

Look for these and many more from Three Ravens Publishing!

Follow us at www.threeravenspublishing.com

You can also find these other fine titles by William Joseph Roberts on Amazon
<u>Flux Runners</u>

What if tomorrow, you tasted freedom for the first time, but that freedom came with a cost... After a government-sanctioned privateering mission goes sideways, the crew of the Betty finds themselves fighting for their lives, light-years from home. Prepare yourself for an adventure with a lovable crew of degenerates and misfits as they dive into the dark unknown....

Wildcat: Foreclosure of a Dream

On the run in a Fallen World...

Three long years after the world Fell, Wildcat Leander Calloway Toler, a deputized lawman—or what passes for one in this Fallen World—finds himself being pursued across the Appalachian wastes with the daughter of a wealthy businessman in tow. Trapped and outgunned, Leander learns that those who took his family and left him for dead in the chaotic days after the Fall have returned.

Infuriated by the bureaucracy of a corrupt system, Leander decides to take matters into his own hands and recruits a team of loyal companions. When they set out on a quest across the mountainous coalfields of southern West Virginia, though, they find out the previously two-bit biker gang has established an empire beyond what anyone could have imagined.

Military scout teams, mutant critters, and radiation zombies are nothing compared to the challenges and pain awaiting Leander once he finds himself in the heart of the Brotherhood's compound, face to face with JalCom…and quite possibly the devil himself.

With the help of Evelyn, an Obsidian agent he finds in the depths of the JalCom lab hidden far below the Greenbriar, can Leander and his team of loyal companions find his family and stop the Brotherhood's reign of terror?

Short Stories by William Joseph Roberts

Appendix A

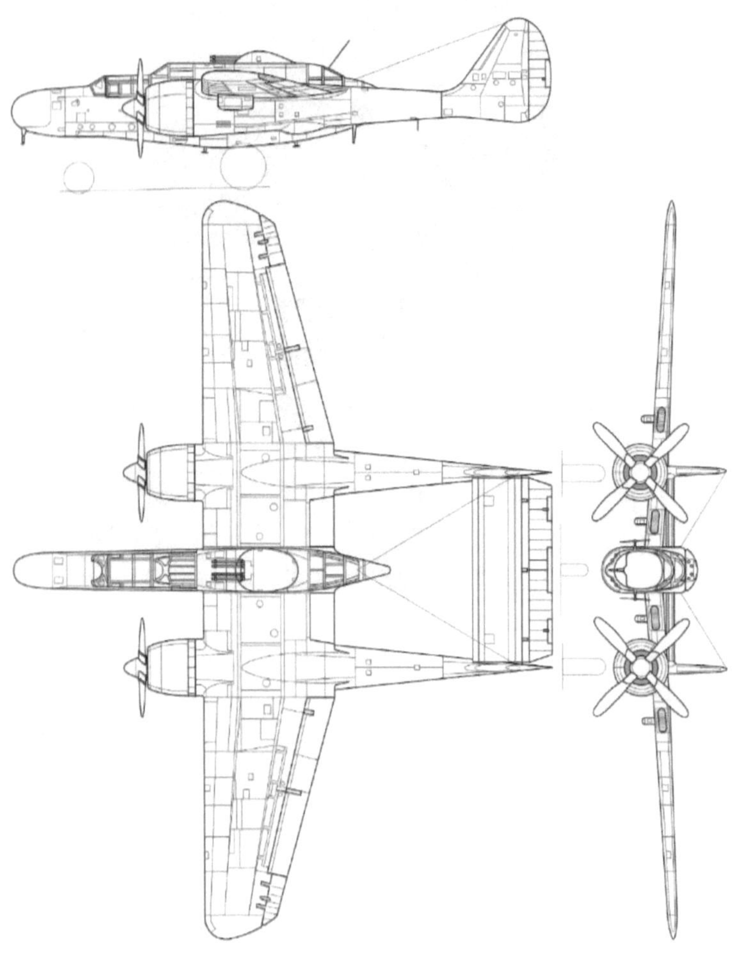

General characteristics of the Northrop P-61 Black Widow

- **Crew:** 2–3 (pilot, radar operator, optional gunner)
- **Length:** 49 ft 7 in (15.11 m)
- **Wingspan:** 66 ft 0 in (20.12 m)
- **Height:** 14 ft 8 in (4.47 m)
- **Wing area:** 662.36 ft² (61.53 m²)
- **Empty weight:** 23,450 lbs. (10,637 kg)
- **Loaded weight:** 29,700 lbs. (13,471 kg)
- **Max. takeoff weight:** 36,200 lbs. (16,420 kg)
- **Fuel capacity:**
  - **Internal:** 640 gal (2,423 L) of AN-F-48 100/130-octane rating gasoline
  - **External:** Up to four 165 gal (625 L) or 310 gal (1,173 L) tanks under the wings
- **Powerplant:** 2 × Pratt & Whitney R-2800-65W Double Wasp radial engines, 2,250 hp (1,680 kW) each
- **Propellers:** four-bladed Curtiss Electric propeller, 1 per engine
  - **Propeller diameter:** 146 in (3.72 m)

Performance

- **Maximum speed:** 366 mph (318 kn, 589 km/h) at 20,000 ft (6,095 m)
- **Combat range:** 1350 mi (1173 nmi, 2172 km)
- **Ferry range:** 1,900 mi (1,650 nmi, 3,060 km) with four external fuel tanks
- **Service ceiling:** 33,100 ft (10,600 m)

Widowmakers

- **Rate of climb:** 2,540 ft/min (12.9 m/s)
- **Wing loading:** 45 lb/ft² (219 kg/m²)
- **Power/mass:** 0.15 hp/lb (250 W/kg)
- **Time to altitude:** 12 min to 20,000 ft (6,100 m) (1,667 ft/min)

Armament

- **Guns:**
  - 4 × 20 mm (.79 in) Hispano AN/M2 cannon in ventral fuselage, 200 rounds per gun
  - 4 × .50 in (12.7 mm) M2 Browning machine guns in remotely operated, full-traverse upper turret, 560 rpg
- **Bombs:** for ground attack, four bombs of up to 1,600 lbs. (726 kg) each or six 5 in (127 mm) HVAR unguided rockets could be carried under the wings. Some aircraft could also carry one 1,000 lbs. (454 kg) bomb under the fuselage.

Avionics

- SCR-720 (AI Mk.X) search radar
- SCR-695 tail warning radar